The Lost Pony of Riverdale

Amanda Wills

For Adrian, Oliver and Thomas.

CHAPTER 1

Poppy McKeever hoped with a passion that she was dreaming. Her family was sitting around the kitchen table looking at her, their faces full of smiling expectation, yet she felt nothing. She looked at each of them in turn, willing herself to feel something – anything – so she could join their happy trio. Her dad was treating her to his full-wattage BBC beam, her stepmother's cerulean blue eyes were appealing for her approval and her brother was fidgeting on his chair, barely able to keep a lid on his excitement. And still she felt nothing. She chewed her bottom lip and wondered how best to break the news.

"I'm sorry," she said at last. "I'm not going."

Her dad and stepmother exchanged a look and Charlie stood up so quickly his chair rocked back and landed on the tiled floor with a clatter that sent

Magpie, their overweight black and white cat, scurrying for cover. Poppy used the diversion to sneak another look at the estate agent's brochure on the table. The pictures showed a cottage sitting squarely at the end of a long gravel drive. Its walls were built from uncompromising grey stone and two dormer windows jutted out of the heavy slate roof like a pair of bushy eyebrows. The yellow paint on the small front door was flaking.

"It looks like an old woman's house. And anyway, it's too far away," she muttered crossly, although her dad and Caroline were too busy with Charlie to hear.

Poppy slid down her chair until she was almost eye-level with the table and regarded her family. It was alright for them, she thought mutinously. They all loved an adventure and couldn't understand why she clung like a limpet to the status quo. But eleven-year-old Poppy knew from bitter experience how someone's life could be turned upside down in a heartbeat. It was only natural that she hated change.

Her dad had dropped the bombshell after dinner. He'd put on his special fake newsreader's voice. Usually his imitations were so over the top they made Poppy giggle. Not today.

"Welcome to the six o'clock news. Here are the headlines. It's all change for the McKeever family -" he began.

Charlie interrupted the broadcast. "Why? Are you getting divorced?" The question was asked with relish. Half his friends at school had parents who'd split up. To six-year-old Charlie it meant having two bedrooms and a constant supply of guilt-induced presents. But her dad and Caroline couldn't keep the grins off their faces. They were even holding hands, for goodness' sake. Whatever the news was, it wasn't a divorce.

"No, you ghoulish boy, we are not getting divorced. It's good news. The McKeever family is leaving leafy Twickenham behind to begin a new life in the country!" her dad announced, squeezing Caroline's hand and smiling encouragingly at the children.

"Cool!" whooped Charlie, his fist punching the air.

"*What*?" Poppy demanded. Surely they weren't serious?

"We've bought a cottage in Devon, right on the edge of Dartmoor. I know it's a surprise but we didn't want to get your hopes up until everything was signed and sealed," her dad said.

Under the table Poppy pinched her thigh. Her worst fears were confirmed. She was definitely awake. "But I like living here. I don't want to move."

"Don't be silly – you'll love living on Dartmoor. It'll be a new start for us all," her dad added, giving Poppy a meaningful look. She wriggled uncomfortably in her chair. She knew exactly what he was referring to. But moving to the other end of the country wasn't going to miraculously make things better between her and Caroline. She hid behind her long fringe and said nothing.

3

"The cottage is called Riverdale. It's absolutely beautiful. Look, here are some photos." Caroline pushed the estate agent's brochure towards her. "The woman we're buying from has lived there for years but the house and land were getting too much for her so she decided to sell. We're so lucky to have found it. It must have been fate."

"I don't care about fate. I don't want to leave Twickenham. I feel close to Mum here," said Poppy bluntly.

The smiles faded from the three faces in front of her and she felt a prickle of guilt when she saw Caroline's wounded expression.

Then her dad dropped a second bombshell.

"You might change your mind when you hear the whole story, Poppy. The house has a sitting tenant."

Curious in spite of herself, Poppy asked grumpily, "What do you mean?"

"The owner of the cottage is moving to a warden-assisted flat. She has an ancient pony and as part of the sale we had to agree that he could stay at Riverdale."

Poppy had a stubborn streak and had been fully prepared to dig her heels in over the move but suddenly all her objections melted away like frost on a sunny winter's morning.

She sat up in her chair. "A pony? What's his name? How big is he? Is he too old to ride?"

"I don't know, sweetheart, the estate agent was a bit vague. And the pony was at the vet's when we looked around the house so we didn't get to meet him, quiz him about his age or take his inside leg measurements."

Poppy played with a strand of her hair and thought. Their house in Twickenham was the last link with her mum. It was a connection she guarded fiercely. And yet waiting for her at this shabby-looking cottage in the middle of nowhere was the one thing she had dreamed of all her life – her own pony. She took another look at the photos. One showed two fields either side of the drive and a ramshackle crop of outbuildings at the back. On closer inspection she noticed something she hadn't seen at first. In one of the fields there was a blurry grey blob. The pony was too far away for Poppy to make out any details, but in her imagination he became the 14.2hh dappled grey of her dreams.

"But you can't ride, Poppy. You've never even sat on a horse!" an incredulous Charlie cried. Some people are born diplomats. Poppy's blond, blue-eyed half-brother was not one of them. Tact had never been one of his strong points. But as usual he was spot on.

"It doesn't matter. I could soon learn. Anyway, I know more about them than you do," she retorted.

That was true at least. Poppy had an almost encyclopaedic knowledge of horses. One of her most prized possessions was a dog-eared box-set collection of books about riding and pony care that she'd unearthed at the bottom of a box of junk at a boot fair the previous summer. Inside the shabby green cardboard case were four well-thumbed books that had helped feed her obsession. Thanks to the books Poppy knew exactly how to look after a pony, in theory at least, from worming him to making a poultice. She knew the difference between a snaffle bit and a kimblewick, a running and a standing martingale. She'd memorised the chapters on teaching horses to jump and riding across country. And this was despite the fact that the closest she'd ever been to riding was having a turn on the donkeys at the beach in Broadstairs.

"I assume that means you're coming with us?" said her dad cheerfully. With an imperceptible nod of the head Poppy stood up and walked out of the kitchen with as much dignity as she could muster after her complete about-turn.

Three months later Poppy pulled the final cardboard box towards her, tore off one last strip of brown parcel tape and carefully stuck the lid down. She looked around her bedroom. There was hardly a square foot of carpet that wasn't covered in boxes. Otherwise the room was bare. All her worldly possessions were packed and ready to go. Her clothes for the morning – a pair of faded jeans and her favourite sweatshirt – were folded neatly on yet another box at the end of the bed. Her dad wanted to leave straight after breakfast to avoid the worst of the traffic. Poppy still wasn't sure she wanted to leave at all, but she hadn't really had a say in the matter. Her dad and Caroline had decided that life in the country would be much better for the children. Healthier, safer, more like the childhoods they remembered, they kept telling her.

She picked up the battered Mickey Mouse clock from her bedside table and set the alarm for seven. Her eyes fell on the photo next to the clock. Taken shortly before her fourth birthday, it could have been one of those pictures newspapers use after a tragedy, with the caption *'In happier times'*. It was winter and their small garden was blanketed under a layer of powdery snow. Poppy and her mum had spent the morning building a snowman. His head was slightly wonky and he was wearing the policeman's helmet from Poppy's dressing up box at a rakish angle. Poppy and her mum were standing to attention either side of him. They were wrapped up in coats, hats and gloves, their usually pale faces rosy with exertion. They were both laughing into the camera. Her dad must have said something funny at the exact moment he had clicked the shutter but Poppy couldn't remember what it was. In fact she wasn't sure if she could even remember her mum with any clarity any more. Photos were a physical reminder of her features but when Poppy tried to visualise Isobel the image was too fleeting to evoke the sound of her voice, the feel of her touch, what she was like. She sighed, picked up the photo, wrapped it in an old scarf and put it in her rucksack, ready for the morning.

As she climbed into bed Poppy thought about their new life in Devon. Her head was a tangled mess of sadness, trepidation and excitement that she was too tired to unravel tonight. Magpie landed with a soft thump beside her. He circled around on the duvet making himself comfortable before finally settling down. Tomorrow life was going to change forever. It was Poppy's last thought before she fell into a dreamless sleep to the sound of Magpie purring.

CHAPTER 2

Poppy was up before six, woken by the butterflies in her stomach. She could hear Caroline singing along softly to a song on the radio in the kitchen below. She dressed quickly and went downstairs. Caroline smiled as she came in and flicked the kettle on.

"Hello, sweetheart. You're up early. I couldn't sleep either. I've been awake since five. There's only toast, I'm afraid. Everything else is packed and ready to go."

"Toast is fine," said Poppy, brushing her long fringe out of her eyes. "Where's Dad?"

"In the shower. And Charlie's still asleep. I'm making the most of the peace and quiet to get the last few jobs done."

Caroline busied herself making toast, her back to Poppy. "How are you feeling about the move? I know it'll be hard to say goodbye to the house but you'll love Riverdale, I promise."

How did Caroline know what she would love and what she wouldn't, Poppy thought, aggrieved. She said nothing. Misinterpreting her silence for sadness, Caroline continued, "And I know you'll miss your friends, especially Hannah, but you can keep in touch by email and phone and she can come to stay in the holidays if her mum agrees."

"Maybe," Poppy muttered, through a mouthful of toast. She knew Caroline was making an effort to talk and she was being monosyllabic in return, but she couldn't help herself. It was the way it had always been. There was a time when Poppy had been chatty, carefree and confident in the knowledge that she was at the centre of her parents' world. Not any more. Her mum had been gone for almost seven years and these days she had both Caroline and Charlie competing for her dad's attention. No matter how hard Caroline tried to include Poppy she felt like she'd been sidelined, left forgotten on a lonely railway siding like one of Charlie's wooden trains. She finished her breakfast, took her plate over to the sink and dashed upstairs to clean her teeth before Caroline could say any more.

Six hours later the McKeevers were stuck in crawling traffic on the A303, in the wake of their lumbering removal lorry. Poppy had lost count of the number of times Charlie had asked if they were nearly there. She stared out of the window, daydreaming about cantering along grassy tracks and soaring over huge cross country fences, a set of pricked grey ears in front of her. Her dad and Caroline were arguing about his next assignment - an eight week posting to the Middle East. Her dad was a war correspondent for the BBC. A familiar face on the news, he reported from the frontline of the world's most dangerous trouble spots, from Iraq to Syria. Wearing his trademark beige flak jacket and often over the sound of distant shell-fire, Mike McKeever brought the horrors of war into people's front rooms from Land's End to John O'Groats. He was due to leave Riverdale the following afternoon.

"Why do you have to go so soon? Couldn't you have at least arranged to have a week off to help with the move? I don't know if I'm going to be able to do it all on my own." Caroline's usually calm voice rose as she turned to face her husband.

"I know, I'm sorry. You'll be fine. I'll be back before you've even realised I've gone."

"By which time it'll all be sorted. As usual," she grumbled.

Poppy was proud of her dad but she missed him desperately when he was away. She'd much rather he was a postman, or a mechanic, or worked in a bank. Anything really, as long as it meant he'd be safe and home for tea every night.

Fields gave way to houses as they approached Plymouth. They followed the removal lorry as it turned off the A38 onto the Tavistock road, the final leg of the journey. Riverdale was a thirty minute drive from the market town and by 3pm they were nearing their destination, the village of Waterby.

"We need to take the second right after the church," reminded Caroline. They drove straight on for a mile and a half and then turned left down a track just past a postbox. "Look, kids - there it is!"

Poppy's first impression of Riverdale was of a slate-roofed stone building with an almost melancholy air, which stood in the shadow of a small tor. The car had barely crunched to a halt on the gravel drive before she had undone her seatbelt, itching to be the first out. As she slammed her door shut behind her she heard Charlie's gleeful tone, "Mum! Magpie's just been sick all over his basket. Yuck, that's so gross!"

"You've found us then! I was beginning to think you'd got lost." Poppy spun round at the sound of a disembodied voice that appeared to be coming from the wooden porch at the front of the house. "I'm Tory Wickens. Welcome to Riverdale!"

A white-haired woman whose face was hatched with a lifetime of wrinkles stepped slowly out of the porch with the aid of two sticks. "I wanted to be here to welcome you to Riverdale. Couldn't say goodbye to the old place without seeing who was taking it on. And you must be Poppy. You'll no doubt be wanting to meet Chester. I need to show you how he likes things done."

Her dad had parked the car and he and Caroline came up and shook the woman's hand. They started chatting about the journey while Charlie struggled to pull Magpie's basket out of the car and Poppy paced impatiently from foot to foot.

"Can we please go and see the pony now?" she asked, after what seemed like a lifetime of pointless talk about whether the A303 was quicker than the motorway.

"Pony? Oh, you must mean Chester. Of course, silly me," said Tory. She beckoned Poppy through the open front door.

The photos of Riverdale hadn't done the house justice, Poppy realised as she followed Tory along the hallway. There were doors leading off the hall to a lounge and a dining room. Both rooms were empty but light streamed in through tall windows and Poppy could see dust motes whirling in the shafts of sunlight. Floral sprigged wallpaper was peeling in places and there were darker rectangles where Tory's pictures must have once hung. But the rooms were large and felt homely despite the faded decor. Tory continued her slow progress through the hall to the kitchen. There was a pillar box red range in the chimney breast and dark oak units lined the walls. The back door was straight ahead and Poppy felt her pulse quicken as they stepped through it to the outbuildings at the back of the house. Like the house, the buildings were built of stone and tiled with slate.

"There are two stables and a small barn where you can store hay and straw. There's enough in there to tide you over for a month or two. That door between the two stables leads to the tack and feed room. It's only small but it's plenty big enough for Chester's things," Tory said.

She saw the barely suppressed excitement on Poppy's face, smiled and pointed to the stable on the left. "That's Chester's stable. I've just given him some hay. Why don't you go and say hello."

Poppy walked the few steps to the stable door. The upper section was wide open and a horseshoe had been tacked to the wooden beam above it. A leather headcollar hung on a hook to the right of the door. The sun felt warm on Poppy's back as she leant over the closed bottom half of the door and peered into the gloom beyond. Straw was banked up around the walls of the stable and she could make out a metal rack on the wall that was half-filled with hay. It took a few seconds for Poppy's eyes to totally adjust to the darkness and when they did she thought she must be imagining things. She looked into the shadows again. Inside the stable, munching on the hay, was not a dappled grey 14.2hh pony but a small, hairy, long-eared donkey.

"But where's Chester?" Poppy asked Tory.

"That's him, pet. That's my Chester. He's a beauty, isn't he?" the old woman replied proudly. At the sound of their voices the donkey turned around, saw Poppy's silhouette over the stable door, curled his top lip and gave an almighty hee-haw.

CHAPTER 3

Disbelief and disappointment swept over Poppy. She felt Tory looking at her, the old woman's snowy eyebrows raised in concern. Tory watched the expression on Poppy's face change from excitement to shock. The girl looked crushed.

"Did you think Chester was a pony? Oh, love, he's my donkey. I've had him since he was a foal. I've told him all about you. He's very pleased that you're going to be looking after him from now on." Tory called softly to the donkey, who came over and nuzzled her outstretched hand.

Tears threatening, Poppy mumbled an apology and ran back through the house and out of the front door. Charlie was sitting on the doorstep with the cat basket on his lap, talking to Magpie. Her dad had started unloading the car and Caroline was issuing orders to the removal men.

"Dad - you said there was a pony here. It's a donkey! You lied to me! How could you?" The lump in her throat stopped her saying any more but tears started sliding down her cheeks. She brushed them away with the back of her hand.

"A donkey! A donkey! Poppy's pony's a donkey! Wait until Hannah finds out! Serves you right for being such a show-off," crowed Charlie from behind Magpie's basket.

"Charlie, that's enough. Poppy, I don't understand. The estate agent was a bit vague but he definitely said it was a pony, at least I thought he did."

Poppy refused to meet her dad's eyes as she kicked the ground viciously. Caroline broke the silence. "Still, a donkey - how sweet. I know we were all expecting a pony but surely a donkey is better than nothing?"

Poppy rounded on her stepmother. "You don't understand. You never do! What use is a donkey? I can't ride that - I'd be a laughing stock. I hate you!"

Shocked by the venom of Poppy's outburst, Caroline flinched and turned away. Poppy stormed off down the drive, her back rigid with tension. Halfway down the track she paused for a moment before climbing over a five bar gate into the larger of Riverdale's two paddocks. She headed towards the far side of the field, where grass gave way to a band of thick woodland. She needed to get as far away as possible. Once she'd reached the post and rail fence that marked Riverdale's boundary she sat down, facing the trees.

Poppy knew better than most how unfair life could be and if she was being honest she knew this latest disappointment wasn't the end of the world. As her dad was fond of saying, worse things happen at sea. Yet she felt bereft. All her life she had fantasised about having her own pony. While some children had imaginary friends, Poppy had had an imaginary Welsh Mountain pony called Smudge when she was younger. She'd made him a stable behind the shed at the bottom of the garden and spent hours constructing cross country courses using bricks and bamboo canes. Eventually she outgrew Smudge but she never outgrew her passion. Some of the luckier girls at school had riding lessons every Saturday morning and she'd eavesdropped conversations about their exploits and the different ponies they rode, longing to be just like them. Her best friend Hannah wasn't interested in horses. She wanted to be a pop star when she grew up and couldn't understand Poppy's fixation. Then her dad had told her about the pony at Riverdale and she'd spent the last three months believing that her dream was finally going to come true. How stupid she'd been.

Half an hour later her dad came to find her.

"I thought I'd give you time to calm down," he said mildly, sitting on the grass beside her. Poppy still felt a huge weight of disappointment but now she'd cooled off it was tinged with shame at her outburst, which she knew had been totally uncalled for. She'd felt an instant liking for Tory and the old woman must have thought she was a spoilt London brat. And Poppy felt increasingly uncomfortable when she remembered how hard she'd been on Caroline.

"Tory's been asking after you. She feels that it's somehow her fault. And Caroline was only trying to cheer you up. There was no need to take it out on her, Poppy."

Her dad looked tired and Poppy felt mortified. She hated upsetting him.

"I'm sorry, Dad. I'll go and apologise to them both. It's just - it's just I was so excited. And now there's nothing for me here. I'd rather be in Twickenham."

"Don't be silly, of course there is. For starters, you need to come and learn how to look after Chester. You wouldn't leave him at the mercy of your brother would you?"

Poppy managed a weak smile. "No, I suppose not. Charlie would probably end up using him for jousting practice or something. You go first. I'll be over in a minute."

She sat for a few moments more, thinking about Chester the donkey and the pony that never was. One day she'd probably be able to laugh at the afternoon's turn of events, but not quite yet. She took a deep breath and prepared to face the music.

As Poppy stood up and brushed the dust from her jeans something caught her eye and she glanced into the wood. She thought she saw a flash of white in the trees. She paused, looked again, but there was nothing there except dark brown, tightly woven branches, heavy with leaves. Shrugging her shoulders she set off back across the field to the house.

CHAPTER 4

By tea-time the removal men had unloaded all the furniture and Poppy had been overloaded with enough information on Chester's likes and dislikes to write, *The A to Z Encyclopaedia on Donkey Care.'*

"By rights donkeys don't like living on their own but there again Chester has always had -" Tory paused, gave a quick shake of her head and carried on. "You need to turn him out after his breakfast every morning and his stable needs to be mucked out every day. He needs fresh water in his stable every night and you also need to make sure the trough in the field is kept topped up.

"He loves his salt lick and he has a scoop of pony nuts a day, half in the morning and half when you bring him in for the night. There's a sack in the dustbin in the tack room. It'll see you through until you get a chance to go to Baxters'. That's the animal feed place on the Tavistock road," Tory added, seeing Poppy's puzzled face.

"I've also left you his headcollar and his grooming kit. I've no use for them where I'm going." Tory was leaning heavily on her two sticks and her eyes had grown misty. "Anyway," she said, visibly collecting herself. "Use the dandy brush for his body and the body brush for his head. You might need to take the curry comb to his tail - he's a terrible one for getting knotted in thistles. And you also need to make sure you pick out his feet twice a day. They say a horse is only as good as his feet, and the same goes for donkeys."

Poppy was glad of her books. At least she'd be able to work out which brush was which. But Tory hadn't quite finished. "He'll also need his feet trimming once every couple of months. He's not due for six weeks but I've left the farrier's phone number with your mum."

"Caroline's not my mum, she's my stepmother," Poppy replied automatically. Tory looked at the thin, pale-faced girl and felt a wave of sympathy. It must have been a rollercoaster of a day. "Here's Chester's headcollar. Why don't I show you how to put it on and you can have a go at grooming him. He'd like that," she said.

The donkey came up, nuzzled Poppy and obligingly held his head perfectly still while she grappled with the leather straps and, under Tory's directions, put the headcollar on. As she picked up the dandy brush and started tackling the donkey's thick grey coat she asked, "What did you mean when you said earlier that Chester wasn't on his own?"

"Nothing for you to worry about, pet."

Poppy could have sworn the old woman suddenly looked shifty, although she had no idea why. The rhythmic sweeping of the dandy brush and Chester's occasional friendly nudges had a calming effect and for the first time that afternoon Poppy felt her spirits rise.

"I really am sorry about before. I didn't mean to be so ungrateful. And I promise I'll look after Chester properly."

"I know you will, pet. I'll go back to the flat happy now I know he's in good hands. I'll miss both him and -" she looked over towards the woods and stopped abruptly.

"Well, it would be lovely if you could come and visit Chester - and me. It would be nice to have a friend here," Poppy told the old woman.

"I'd like that, pet. And you're always welcome to come and see me in my rabbit-hutch of a flat. But be careful of Mrs Parker. She's the warden and she's a formidable character. I've rubbed her up the wrong way already and I've only been there five minutes."

They spent the next hour working together companionably, grooming and feeding Chester and settling him down for the evening. With Tory guiding her, Poppy picked out the donkey's feet and untangled at least five burrs from his tail. By the time they'd finished Tory's nephew had arrived to drive her back to her new flat. Clasping Poppy's hand as she stood propped up on her sticks by his car Tory said, "Goodbye Poppy, see you soon. And thank you for looking after Chester. He means the world to me."

Poppy smiled. "Thank you for letting him stay at Riverdale. He can be my pretend pony. Who needs the real thing anyway?"

Charlie was unpacking his action heroes in the hall and Caroline was busy finishing tea when Poppy returned indoors.

"Your dad's upstairs making up our beds. Why don't you come and help me lay the table. Dinner will be ready in a minute," said Caroline, drying her hands on a tea-towel.

Poppy looked at her stepmother. Caroline was tall, blonde and blue-eyed - the polar opposite of Poppy's mum, Isobel, who had been green-eyed, dark and petite. Poppy knew deep-down that Caroline wasn't your archetypical wicked stepmother. She was kind and patient and always put the children first, but from the first day her dad had introduced them Poppy had felt prickly and defensive. She couldn't even begin to explain why. But she noticed the way Caroline would suddenly scoop Charlie up into a hug, smothering his apple-pink cheeks with butterfly kisses. She tried not to feel jealous when Caroline tickled her irrepressible brother until giggles convulsed his whole body or when she stroked his hair absentmindedly while she was reading the paper or watching television. The pair had such a close bond and they strongly resembled her fair-haired father. Poppy, who was the spitting image of Isobel, felt like the cuckoo in the nest.

As she leant over to unpack the knives and forks from one of the dozen or so cardboard boxes in the kitchen, a fan of dark hair hiding her face, Poppy mumbled an apology to Caroline. Fortunately her stepmother wasn't one to hold a grudge.

"That's OK, sweetheart. Your dad and I were just worried about you. I know how excited you were about the pony. Right, let's get this show on the road. Can you tell the boys dinner's ready?"

Before she went to bed in her new room at the back of the house, Poppy slipped out to say goodnight to Chester. It was a still night and the silence felt alien after the 24-7 noise of London. The donkey was quietly munching on some hay but when he saw Poppy's head poke over his stable door he came over and gave her a nudge.

"Tory said you like Polos. I'll make sure we get some tomorrow. Do you miss her?" Poppy asked, as she stroked the donkey's velvety nose. The expression in his soft brown eyes was unreadable but he gave her another nudge, as if to say, 'Yes, of course I miss her, but you'll do,' and Poppy felt a mixture of gratitude and protectiveness towards her new charge. An owl hooted, followed by the distant sound of a horse neighing. Chester lifted his head and gave a plaintiff hee-haw in return.

"Must be one of the Dartmoor ponies. I didn't realise they would be so close," Poppy said, half to herself. "I'll take Charlie exploring tomorrow. It'll be fun to have real wild ponies on our doorstep." And she kissed Chester's nose, crept back into the house and took herself off to bed.

CHAPTER 5

The first thing Poppy saw when she opened her eyes the next morning was her favourite photo of her mum. She'd unpacked it the previous night and it was back in pride of place on her bedside table. When Caroline came into her room a few minutes later, Poppy was lying on her side, staring at the picture with such a look of yearning on her face that Caroline felt the familiar jolt of inadequacy somewhere deep in her stomach.

"Breakfast's nearly ready and it's a beautiful morning!" she said brightly, pulling open Poppy's curtains to reveal a cloudless blue sky. "What are you going to do today? I need to drive into Tavistock and hit the supermarket but you two can stay at home if you want. Your dad'll be here getting ready for his trip - the flight's at eight tonight so he's going to need to leave by three."

"Um, I thought Charlie and I might spend the morning exploring properly. I heard a neigh last night so I think we must have a herd of Dartmoor ponies quite close. I want to see if we can find them," said Poppy, as she swung her legs out of bed and reached for her jeans.

"Good idea. Make sure he stays out of trouble. I could do without a trip to casualty today." Poppy nodded. If there was a tree to fall out of or a river to fall into Charlie was always the first to oblige. As a result he'd been a frequent visitor to the accident and emergency department at West Middlesex University Hospital.

When she suggested to Charlie that they spend the morning exploring together his blue eyes shone with excitement.

"Cool! Can I bring my Nerf gun, just in case we meet any predators?"

"No! You'll give the Dartmoor ponies a heart attack! They'll never let us near them," shrieked Poppy, who was beginning to doubt the wisdom of inviting him along.

"Some people say there are big cats living wild on Dartmoor you know. Dad told me," Charlie said, sticking out his chin.

"Maybe, but the noise you make they'd run a mile anyway. Why don't you bring your bow and arrows instead?" she suggested.

"Alright," he grumbled. "But I have been practising

tracking and stalking. The big cats won't know I'm there until I spring onto their backs." He demonstrated by taking a flying leap from his chair to the back of the nearby sofa. Poppy looked at Caroline and they raised their eyebrows in unison. Charlie's passion for danger was fuelled by his addiction to wildlife and survival programmes. While Poppy followed top riders like Pippa Funnell and Ellen Whitaker and spent hours watching Badminton, Burghley and the Horse of the Year Show, Charlie's heroes were Bear Grylls, Steve Backshall and Ray Mears and his ambition when he grew up was to track and film clouded leopards in the foothills of the Himalayas.

The two set off shortly after Poppy had fed and groomed Chester and turned him out in the smaller paddock to the left of the house. The paddock was bordered by a much larger field of pastureland that belonged to the farm next door and was grazed by a herd of black-faced sheep. There was a public footpath from the road at the bottom of Riverdale's drive leading diagonally across the sheep field and Poppy and Charlie started their exploration by following it. At the far side of the field they came to a second unmade lane that ran parallel to the Riverdale drive but was more roughshod than theirs.

"I didn't notice this driveway yesterday. I bet it leads to the farm Tory told me about. She said a girl about my age lived there," said Poppy.

"Does she have a brother?" asked Charlie, bending

down to inspect the ground, his bow and arrows slung casually across one shoulder. "Yes, that's definitely sheep poo," he said with satisfaction.

"Sherlock Holmes has nothing on you," said Poppy drily, as she looked behind him to the field of sheep. "I don't know if she has a brother, Tory didn't say. She just said I should go over and say hello once we'd settled in."

Poppy would have loved to have been the type of girl who thought nothing of casually rocking up on a stranger's doorstep and introducing herself. Charlie had inherited their dad's gregarious nature and didn't think twice about bowling into new situations and making friends. But Poppy was often paralysed by her shyness. Knowing her luck she'd stand on the farmhouse doorstep and be rendered mute, opening and closing her mouth like a demented goldfish.

They re-traced their steps and crossed the Riverdale drive into the field to the right of the house. It was four times the size of Chester's paddock and in Poppy's opinion was the perfect size for a pony. The field was flanked by the dense woodland that Poppy had seen the day before. Charlie led the way, climbing over the post and rail perimeter fence and disappearing into the trees. Her usually boisterous, noisy brother turned back to look at her, holding his index finger to his lips as he warned her to be quiet. She followed as silently as she could as he led her soundlessly through the undergrowth. Eventually they came to the bank of a gently flowing stream.

"No wonder the house is called Riverdale," whispered Poppy.

"Let's follow the river upstream," breathed Charlie. Life in Devon seemed a long way from suburban Twickenham and the potential for adventure appeared limitless. They came to a bend in the stream where it widened out and the water slowed pace. A small sandy beach in front of them was too much for Charlie to resist and he raced over, pulling off his trainers and socks, whooping with glee as he ran, his silent tracking temporarily forgotten. Poppy joined him and they paddled in the icy water until they couldn't feel their feet. As they sat on a boulder drying their toes Charlie tugged at his sister's sleeve.

"Look, there's a hoofprint from one of your Dartmoor ponies," he said, pointing to the sand in front of them. It was a shallow print, about the size of Poppy's hand, facing the water. The ponies must come here to drink, she thought excitedly.

Charlie seemed to read her mind. "It's like an African watering hole only in Dartmoor. They probably come to drink here at dawn and dusk, like the animals do on the savannah. We could come and watch them one night."

"Fantastic idea, little brother. Shall we carry on?" Charlie nodded in assent and they continued to follow the river. As the trees thinned out, Poppy realised they had reached the moorland at the base of the tor which towered over Riverdale. In front of them was a small herd of seven Dartmoor ponies. Some bay, one chestnut and a couple of greys. When they heard the two children they looked up from their grazing. Before Poppy and Charlie could get any closer they ambled off together around the far side of the tor.

Charlie strode purposefully over to where one of the ponies had been standing and peered down at the ground.

"That's a bit weird. Come and have a look," he beckoned to his sister. The grass was marshy and at first Poppy wasn't sure what she was supposed to be looking at.

Seeing her puzzled face Charlie explained, "Look, see the hoofprints in the mud. They're tiny - much smaller than the one we saw by the river. That must have been made by a bigger pony, maybe even a horse."

Poppy felt a fizz of excitement which made the hairs on the back of her neck stand up. "Very clever. Who needs Steve Backshall when you have ace tracker Charlie McKeever as your guide?" she teased him, wondering whether the mystery hoofprint had anything to do with the flash of white she thought she'd seen in the wood.

"No sign of any big cats though. I wanted to find at least a pawprint - maybe even the carcass of a dead sheep," said Charlie glumly.

Halfway up the tor they found a boulder to sit on and Poppy produced two chocolate bars from the pocket of her sweatshirt. From their vantage point they gazed at their new home, spread out before them in the sunshine.

"I think I'm going to like living here. I thought I'd be missing Twickenham by now but Riverdale almost feels like home already," mused Poppy. Charlie scrambled off the boulder. "Same. Come on, let's go back now. It must be nearly lunchtime. The chocolate was nice but I'm still starving."

By the time they reached the house Caroline was unpacking bags of shopping in the kitchen. Charlie rushed straight in and began regaling her with tales of their morning's adventures. As she walked to and fro finding space in the cupboards for the various jars, tins and packets Caroline occasionally ruffled his thatch of blond hair. Poppy hovered in the doorway, feeling excluded as usual, a feeling that was compounded when her dad came downstairs, joined Caroline and Charlie in the kitchen and started teasing Charlie about his big cat obsession.

Caroline unpacked the last of the shopping and looked over at Poppy. "I overheard a strange conversation when I popped into Waterby Post Office to buy stamps this morning." She described how she'd been standing in the queue behind two old farmworkers. "They were talking about the annual drift. Did you know hundreds of Dartmoor ponies are rounded up off the moor every autumn before being taken to market?"

Poppy nodded. She'd read about the drift in one of her pony magazines. It was a tradition that had been going for generations.

"Anyway," Caroline continued, "One said to the other, 'I wonder if they'll finally manage to round up the Wickens' colt this year.'" Her attempt at a broad Devon accent was met with smiles from her husband and son.

"And the other one said, 'Colt? He must be ten if he's a day.'"

By now Caroline had everyone's attention. "So the first one said he reckoned that the colt must have had help hiding from the drift all these years. And the second one seemed to find that funny because he was laughing when he replied, 'Aye, but what'll happen now that the help is stuck in an old people's flat in Tavistock?' Bit strange, wasn't it?" said Caroline, giving Poppy's shoulder a quick squeeze. Poppy shrugged off her stepmother's hand.

"If you say so," she shrugged again and left the three of them to their game of Happy Families.

CHAPTER 6

All too soon the taxi arrived and it was time to say goodbye. As the driver loaded the bags into the boot Poppy's dad gave her a hug, kissed Caroline and shook Charlie by the hand.

"I'll be back before you know it," he told the three glum faces. That's what he always said, Poppy thought, but it didn't make the time go any quicker.

"Keep smiling, kids, and don't forget to watch the news for the McKeever messages!" he told them. Years ago her dad had developed a secret code meant for the family when he delivered his news reports. Poppy's code was a plaited leather friendship bracelet which, worn on his right wrist, meant he was thinking of her. She'd made it for him when she was eight. A royal blue handkerchief in his breast pocket was Charlie's special message to remind him that he was the man of the house in his absence. He communicated with Caroline by a pair of sunglasses perched on top of his head. Poppy had never been privy to that particular message but she'd noticed that it always made Caroline blush.

He blew them all kisses as the taxi drove away and Poppy, Charlie and Caroline walked back inside, feeling deflated as they always did when he left on an assignment.

"I'm going to design a big cat trap," announced Charlie, setting off upstairs to his bedroom.

"I suppose I'd better make a start on dinner. Want to give me a hand?" Caroline asked Poppy.

She shook her head. "Do you mind if I go and sort out my room? There are boxes everywhere and I can't find anything."

"You go ahead. I'll give you a shout when dinner's ready."

Poppy's bedroom was a perfect square, set in the eaves below the cat-slide roof at the back of the house. From her window she could see the stables and barn with the tor looming darkly in the distance. She looked around the room. The removal men had stacked the boxes in one corner. Caroline had unpacked her clothes and her dad had threaded her fairy lights around the wrought iron bedframe but otherwise the room was bare. She was relieved that Tory's weakness for floral wallpaper and carpets was less pronounced there. She actually thought the delicate flowers, the colour of amethyst, looked pretty against the cream wallpaper. The oatmeal carpet was flecked with brown and opposite the bed was an old cast iron fireplace.

Box by box, Poppy began unpacking her books, photos, posters and mementos, becoming absorbed in her work as gradually the room began to take shape. Her favourite posters were stuck to the walls and books were arranged in a tall, oak bookcase. A patchwork blanket, knitted by Caroline in rainbow colours the previous winter, was carefully folded at the end of her bed and a matching cushion was plumped up on an old wicker chair next to the window.

At the bottom of the final box, protected by layers of bubble wrap, was another boot fair find. The bronze racehorse may have seen better days but Poppy loved it. To her it captured the very essence of freedom and speed. She looked around the room for a suitable home for it and settled on the fireplace. As she placed the galloping thoroughbred on the mantelpiece her fingers brushed against something silky. A tiny triangle of red material protruded from a narrow gap between the mantle and the wall. Poppy tried to pull it out with her fingers but the material was too small and smooth to grip. She thought for a moment then disappeared into the bathroom to ferret around in Caroline's make-up bag. She returned with a pair of tweezers which she used to tease the fabric from its hiding hole.

"Oh!" Poppy exclaimed. It was a red rosette with

the words Brambleton Horse Show in gold lettering around the edge. The ribbon was faded and smelt so musty it made her sneeze. She turned the rosette over. On the back someone had written *September 24, 2006*. Poppy had been four in 2006. She shuddered. It wasn't a year she wanted to remember.

Before she could begin to wonder who the rosette had belonged to she heard her name being called. Caroline poked her head around the bedroom door.

"There's a visitor for you, Poppy," she said.

An auburn head appeared, followed by the body of a girl about Poppy's age, with hazel eyes and a Cheshire cat-sized grin on her face. Poppy stuffed the rosette in her pocket and stared in silence.

"I'm Scarlett," the girl said. "You must be Poppy. Tory told me a girl was moving into her old house and she said I ought to come and say hello once you'd settled in. I live at Ashworthy, it's the farm next door."

Poppy silently thanked Tory for sending the freckle-faced girl to Riverdale. She would never have plucked up the courage to knock on Scarlett's door.

"I'll leave you two to it," Caroline said, retreating downstairs with a satisfied smile on her face. She was aware that other children thought Poppy was aloof, although she knew it was just shyness. A bubbly no-nonsense farmer's daughter was just what Poppy needed to bring her out of herself, Caroline thought.

In the bedroom Scarlett began giving Poppy the third degree.

"What's it like living in London?" she demanded. "Have you been to the Natural History Museum? My brother Alex went there on a school trip once, said it was awesome. What about the London Eye? Did you see any of the Olympics? I would have given my right arm to have gone to Greenwich Park to see the eventing but I had to make do with watching it on the telly. How are you enjoying looking after Chester? He's so sweet - I've known him all my life. Do you ride? I bet the riding schools in London are amazing. They ride in Hyde Park, don't they?"

Poppy was finding it impossible to get a word in edgeways but as Scarlett paused for breath she said shyly, "No, I've never learnt to ride, although I've always wanted to. Do you have a pony?"

"Yes, Alex and I both have Dartmoor ponies, Flynn and Blaze, although Alex is far too big to ride Flynn these days. For the last couple of years he's just been turned out in the field getting fatter and fatter, poor thing. Flynn that is, not Alex!" Scarlett laughed loudly at her own joke. Then she looked around the bedroom, seeing the riding magazines, pony books and posters. "So you obviously love horses."

Poppy nodded.

"But you've never ridden?"

"Only donkey rides on the beach."

Scarlett looked at Poppy with concern. "That's terrible." She paused for a second before a thought struck her. "I know! I could teach you to ride. You'll have the whole summer holidays to learn. Flynn is the perfect gentleman, a proper schoolmaster, he'd look after you beautifully, and goodness knows he needs the exercise."

Poppy's heart soared.

"Yes please," she breathed, all shyness forgotten. "When can we start?"

CHAPTER 7

Poppy had to wait a week until Scarlett's school broke up for the summer before they could begin lessons. Scarlett was also in her final year at primary school and both girls were due to start at the secondary school in Tavistock in September. So Poppy spent the week getting to know Chester. The donkey stood patiently for hours while she practised putting on his headcollar and taking it off again, tying quick release knots and picking out his feet. She gave the tackroom a spring clean, sending spiders scuttling as she brushed away ancient webs. She talked Caroline into driving to Baxters' Animal Feeds and spent a blissful hour among the horse paraphernalia, spending her pocket money on a smart grooming kit for Chester. Caroline bought her a skull cap with a navy and pink silk.

On Saturday morning Poppy walked to Ashworthy along the footpath at the front of Riverdale, her new hat under her arm, feeling equally nervous and excited. She'd spent so many years daydreaming about riding, imagining herself cantering along bridleways with the casualness of a cowgirl or at horse shows being presented with trophies so shiny she could see her face in them. What if she was useless? What if she was so incompetent she never got the hang of it? Taking a deep breath, she knocked on the front door. The sound set off a round of barking and she could hear a boy say, "Meg, be quiet! Oh, I think there's someone at the front door."

When the door opened, Scarlett was standing there clad in jodhpurs and a checked shirt, a smile on her freckled face.

"There you are! We wondered who it was. Only the postman uses the front door. We always go around the back. But how would you know that – it's the first time you've been here. Anyway, come in and you can meet everyone."

Scarlett kept up a stream of chat as she led Poppy through the house. Ashworthy was the kind of farmhouse that Poppy had read about in books but never believed actually existed. The house had low ceilings, mullioned windows and the aroma of baking. It was shabby and threadbare in places but Poppy loved it. Scarlett's mum, Pat, was in the kitchen, chopping vegetables and dropping them into an enormous saucepan which sat like a witch's cauldron on the Rayburn. A black and white border collie appeared, her tail wagging so quickly it was almost a blur. The dog woofed a greeting, pushing a wet nose into Poppy's hand and giving her palm a soggy lick. She stroked the dog's silky ears.

"This is Meg. She seems to like you already. Oh, and that's Mum," added Scarlett as an afterthought.

Pat smiled. "I've heard all about you, Poppy. It's so nice for Scarlett to have someone her age next door. How are you settling in?"

Scarlett's mum was as freckly as her daughter and had the same open, friendly face. Poppy instantly felt at ease. They chatted for a while until Scarlett grew impatient and dragged Poppy outside to meet Flynn and Blaze. Flynn was a rotund, dark bay gelding who made a beeline for Poppy's pockets looking for a titbit. Blaze was a chestnut mare with a flaxen mane and tail, whose fox-red coat matched the exact shade of Scarlett's hair, as if by design.

"Doesn't your brother ride any more?" Poppy asked, as she stroked Flynn's brown nose, trying to calm the butterflies in her stomach.

"He's thirteen," Scarlett said, rolling her eyes, as if his age explained everything. "He used to be fun but these days he's *so* boring. He's only happy when he's got his head in a book. Right, shall we get started?"

Poppy finally summoned the courage to broach an issue that had been bothering her all week. "My stepmum has bought me a hat but I haven't got any jodhpurs or boots." She looked down at her jeans and trainers in despair.

"Minor details. I'm sure we can find some. Mum never throws anything away. You start grooming Flynn and I'll go and ask."

She returned a few minutes later with a pair of Alex's old jodhpurs and boots which fitted well enough and they spent a happy morning with Scarlett teaching her friend how to tack Flynn up, mount and dismount, the correct riding position and how to hold the reins properly. Scarlett clipped a leadrope to Flynn's snaffle bit and led him and Poppy around the farm, giving a running commentary as they walked sedately through fields and along tracks. Poppy felt exhilarated. Flynn was as round as a Thelwell pony but he was alert and forward going and Poppy had the feeling he was enjoying himself as much as she was.

Over the next three weeks Poppy learnt the basics of riding under Scarlett's knowledgeable, albeit occasionally impatient, tutelage. The two girls spent every morning at Ashworthy. For a couple of days, Poppy remained on the lead rein. But eventually Scarlett taught her the aids, how to use her hands, legs and seat to start, halt, back and turn the long-suffering bay gelding. It was the sort of thing that was second nature to Scarlett, who had learned to ride almost before she could walk. By the end of the first week Poppy had fallen off four times but had mastered a sitting and a rising trot, although she was still too nervous to trot without stirrups. After two weeks she had successfully managed a couple of canters and Scarlett was muttering about trotting poles and cavellettis.

"You do have a natural seat," said her friend, looking at Poppy with a critical eye as she sat on Flynn at the end of a lesson. "And I don't mean to sound big-headed, but I do think I'm a born teacher," she added modestly.

"You're a hard taskmaster, that's for sure," replied Poppy, who'd discovered muscles in places she didn't know existed. She had bruises on her backside and blisters on every finger. But despite the aches and pains and occasional falls she was having the time of her life. She'd barely been at home since meeting Scarlett and her newfound friendship eased the loneliness she usually felt when her dad was away.

She'd finally met Scarlett's brother, Alex. Tall and thin, with auburn hair a few shades darker than his sister's, he had mumbled a greeting and not said a word since.

"He's so rude!" Scarlet had complained, although Poppy recognised the signs and suspected he was just shy.

The McKeevers had been at Riverdale for a month when Pat invited them to Sunday lunch. Caroline had spent the first three weeks at their new house in a frenzy of activity, ripping up carpets, sanding and varnishing floorboards, stripping wallpaper and whitewashing walls. After transforming the house she'd started digging a vegetable patch while Charlie spent hours making dens and honing his tracking skills in the fields around Riverdale. Most evenings the children sat with Caroline after dinner and watched the six o'clock news in case their dad was on and every few days he rang from the Middle East for a short chat.

The lunch was a welcome distraction and when they arrived the three McKeevers were greeted by the sight of an enormous joint of Ashworthy lamb served in the centre of a huge pine table, surrounded by dishes of roast potatoes and parsnips and Pat's home-grown vegetables. Charlie was his normal ebullient self, firing questions at Scarlett's dad, Bill. "Can I have a go at shearing one of the sheep? What do you do with all the cow pats? Have you ever seen a big cat?"

"As a matter of fact I think I have," Bill replied between mouthfuls. "It was during lambing last spring. It was so cold there was still snow on some of the higher tors. One night I was out at midnight helping one of the ewes deliver twins. Meg started barking at the line of trees at the edge of the field. I shone my torch over to see what she was fussing about but all I could see was a pair of eyes shining back at me in the torchlight."

Scarlett, Alex and Pat had obviously heard the story a dozen times and carried on eating. Charlie had stopped, his fork raised half-way to his mouth, his eyes as wide as saucers.

"Dad, it was probably just a fox," said Alex. Poppy looked up, surprised – it was the longest sentence she'd heard him utter.

"I know, that's what I told myself. Lord knows I've seen enough foxes in my time. But the eyes were spaced too far apart. And the reaction of the sheep was strange. They ran from that side of the field in a blind panic. I just can't explain it. Anyway, whatever it was disappeared as quickly as it had appeared and I've not seen anything like it since."

Charlie was agog and Poppy could practically see his brain whirring, dreaming up madcap schemes to track down the Beast of Dartmoor.

Talk turned to Riverdale and how the McKeevers were settling in. Caroline seemed subdued, Poppy thought, watching her normally chatty stepmother. She looked tired. Not surprising really. She hadn't stopped since they'd moved to Devon.

"How long did Tory live at Riverdale?" Poppy asked.

"All her married life and then she stayed there on her own after her husband died fifteen years ago. Douglas was a lovely man. It must have been lonely for her but she refused to move into the village," said Pat.

"Did she never have children?" Poppy thought of the red rosette she'd found in her bedroom.

"Yes, she has a daughter, Jo, but they haven't spoken for a long while," Pat answered.

"Why not?" Charlie asked, through a mouthful of roast lamb.

"Nothing for you to worry your head about, love,"

Pat said, as she stood up and started piling second helpings onto everyone's already heaving plates.

After the meal, Poppy and Scarlett were sitting on the post and rail fence around Flynn and Blaze's paddock watching the ponies graze. Poppy asked if her friend knew what had happened to cause the rift between Tory and her daughter.

"No, Mum won't tell me. Says it's none of my business. I asked Tory once but she looked so sad I wished I hadn't. I never asked her again."

The conversation was quickly forgotten as the girls started discussing the next day's lesson, when Scarlett was going to start teaching Poppy how to jump. Flynn, whose rotund belly was beginning to fade away with all the work he was doing, came over and nuzzled their pockets for a Polo.

"Caroline's really cool, you are so lucky to have her as a stepmum," said Scarlett suddenly.

"What?" asked Poppy, who had been wondering how many times she was likely to fall off in her jumping lesson the next morning.

"My mum's great, I know. She's a brilliant cook and I know she loves me but she's stuck in a time warp - she's never even used a computer for goodness sake! Caroline's so fashionable and she knows all about music and stuff. It must be great to have someone like her as a mum."

Poppy looked Scarlett straight in the eye. "I'd rather have my own mum, Scarlett. Caroline doesn't love me, not like she loves Charlie. Not like your mum loves you. Not like my mum loved me."

Her friend took a deep breath and finally asked the question she'd being bursting to ask since the day they met.

"What did happen to your mum, Poppy?"

CHAPTER 8

Poppy had always felt responsible for her mum's death. Although she had difficulty remembering details of her mum's face - the exact shade of her green eyes, the curve of her smile - she had regular flashbacks to the accident in which every agonizing moment played out in her head.

They were walking home from school one bitterly cold afternoon not long after the snowman photo had been taken. Poppy's right hand was clasped safely in her mum's and in her left she held her beloved stuffed rabbit, Ears. They had crossed the main road at the top of their road when Poppy realised she'd dropped the rabbit. She slipped like an eel out of her mum's grasp and darted back into the road to rescue him. Her mum turned and screamed, "Poppy, no!" and ran towards her. Poppy could still remember the look of absolute terror on Isobel's face when she saw a speeding car bearing down on them.

The next few minutes were a blur of disjointed sounds and images. The sickening squeal of brakes as the car shuddered to a halt. A flash of red as her mum was thrown over the bonnet. Howls from the young driver as he realised what he'd done. The screech of sirens as police cars and an ambulance arrived.

Poppy saw her four-year-old self standing at the edge of the road, clutching Ears to her chest, not understanding what had happened. Her mum was lying on the pavement a few feet away. She had run over and tried to shake her awake. But her mum hadn't moved.

"She's sleeping," Poppy told the paramedics over and over again. They gently lifted Isobel onto a stretcher and covered her face with a blanket. Poppy pulled the blanket off. "Don't do that. She won't be able to breathe."

A group of mums and children stood silently watching the paramedics lift the stretcher into the ambulance. A familiar figure burst through them and gathered Poppy into her arms. It was Sarah, Hannah's mum. They usually walked home together, the four of them, but that day Sarah had stopped to speak to one of the teachers about a school trip.

"Where are they taking my mummy?" Poppy asked her.

Sarah's face was wet with tears. "Oh, my darling. Mummy's badly hurt. They've got to take her to hospital. You can come home with us and I'll phone your daddy."

For once Scarlett was silent as Poppy recounted the events of that day.

"I still thought she would be OK," Poppy remembered. "No-one told me what had really happened. My dad was in Iraq at the time and it was two days before they could find the Army unit he was based with and tell him about the accident. He flew straight home but it felt like ages before he got back."

Isobel had taken the full force of the impact protecting Poppy from the car. Countless well-meaning bereavement counsellors had told Poppy over the following months that it wasn't her fault. She didn't believe any of them.

"After all, if I hadn't run into the road my mum wouldn't have died, would she?" Poppy said flatly.

Scarlett didn't know how to answer so tried to change the subject. "How did your dad meet Caroline?"

Poppy gazed towards the moor. "He refused to go abroad for the first year after Mum died so he could be at home for me. I had a childminder called Shirley who looked after me before and after school and in the holidays, but Dad was home every night. Then Caroline started working at the BBC. He said they became friends first and then he realised he was falling in love." Poppy pulled a face. "He started inviting her around to our house. She tried to be friendly, but she wasn't Mum. I hated seeing them together. One day he picked me up from school, took me to our favourite cafe, bought me a milkshake and told me he had some 'exciting' news. Caroline was having a baby and he'd asked her to marry him."

At Caroline's insistence Poppy had been the bridesmaid at their wedding. Dressed from head to toe in cream silk to match Caroline's elegant wedding dress, Poppy had spent the entire day missing her mum while all around her were smiling and celebrating her dad's second chance at happiness.

"Then Charlie was born, Caroline gave up work to be at home with us and my dad started going away for work again. I always felt like the odd one out but when it was just the three of us it was even worse. Luckily there was always Hannah."

"She was your best friend in Twickenham?" Scarlett asked, trying not to feel jealous. "Does she ride?"

Poppy laughed, "No, horses are far too muddy and she'd hate mucking out. She hasn't even got a pair of wellies. Hannah's ambition is to win X-Factor. But we've been best friends since forever." The last remark was more to convince herself than Scarlett. Poppy had emailed Hannah once or twice a week since the move to Riverdale but whereas her emails were filled with the exploits of Flynn, Blaze and Chester, walks on the moor with Scarlett and Charlie and updates on the house and Caroline's fledgling vegetable patch, Hannah talked about clothes she had bought, music she was listening to and her new group of friends. As the days flew by they grew further and further apart. Poppy supposed it was bound to happen.

She glanced at Scarlett, who was chewing on a piece of grass. Bubbly, generous Scarlett, who had welcomed her into her life with open arms. Poppy felt lucky to have found such a good friend.

"To be honest, I have much more in common with you than I do with Hannah these days. At least we're as pony-mad as each other. And you don't want to be a pop star, do you?"

Scarlett grinned and shook her head vehemently. "I can't imagine anything worse. I'd love to win Badminton maybe, but not X-Factor." Her face became solemn and she said quietly, "Thank you for telling me about your mum, Poppy. I'm so sorry about what happened. But you really mustn't blame yourself. It was the driver's fault, not yours."

Poppy looked unconvinced. But Scarlett's next words threw her completely.

"Caroline does love you, you know. It's completely obvious to me. Surely you can see it too?"

"You're barking up the wrong tree there. She puts up with me because she has to. No more than that."

CHAPTER 9

Charlie's obsession with big cats was growing by
the day. With Poppy's help he'd Googled news stories
of reported sightings on Dartmoor and was
convinced Bill hadn't seen a fox while lambing the
previous spring.

"It could have been a puma or a jaguar, or maybe
even a panther, which is another name for a black
leopard," he informed Poppy and Caroline over
breakfast one day towards the end of August. The
holiday was slipping through the children's fingers
like sand and they only had a dozen days left before
they started at their new schools.

"Poppy," whispered Charlie, as Caroline bent down
to empty the dishwasher. "It's going to be a full moon
tonight. Can we go to the river later, see who turns up
for a drink?" He winked conspiratorially at her.

"OK, little brother. I'll come along and hold your hand, in case there are any beasties about," she smiled.

For the rest of the day Charlie was fizzing with excitement. Caroline was suspicious. "I know he's up to something. You don't know what he's planning do you? I've got a horrible feeling it's something to do with this wretched big cat he's convinced is living on the doorstep."

Poppy couldn't hold her stepmother's gaze as she replied evasively, "I don't know. He hasn't mentioned anything to me."

"Sweetheart, you would tell me if you knew, wouldn't you? I don't want him to do anything silly."

"Don't worry. I promise I'll keep an eye on him." That much was true, at least.

"Thank-you, darling," said Caroline, giving Poppy such a sweet smile she felt the usual twinge of resentment. Caroline was never as worried about her safety as she was about Charlie's.

That evening Charlie went straight to bed without any of his usual time-wasting tactics, adding to Caroline's unease. But she was too glued to the ten o'clock news watching Mike's poignant report on a suicide bomber who'd destroyed a school in Afghanistan to hear the click of the back door as the two children let themselves out.

Charlie had insisted they both cover their faces with the camouflage face paints that their dad had brought home from one of his trips to the Middle

East. He'd been given them by a British soldier he'd interviewed in the desert.

"I knew they'd come in handy one day," whispered the six-year-old, his face streaked with brown and khaki-green, his ultramarine eyes glittering with excitement.

It was a cloudless night and the full moon cast a benevolent light on the pair as Poppy once again followed her brother across the field, over the fence and into the wood.

This time, in place of his bow and arrow, Charlie carried a pair of bird-watching binoculars around his neck and the small digital camera he'd been given for Christmas in his pocket. The spindly beams of light cast by their head torches helped them pick their way through the undergrowth until they reached the river. They turned left to follow it upstream, scrambling over fallen branches until they came to the bend where the river widened out.

Before they reached the small sandy beach Charlie stopped, motioning Poppy to follow suit.

"We don't want to get too close," he murmured. "We need to find somewhere good to hide."

Poppy looked around, her gaze settling on a fallen oak tree with a girth so wide they could easily take cover behind it. She pointed and they crept silently towards it, slithered over the tree and positioned themselves as comfortably as they could behind it. Charlie grinned at Poppy and pointed at the luminous dial of his wristwatch. It was ten to eleven and

Caroline was probably in bed by now, oblivious to their exploits.

At first it was exciting listening to the sounds of the night and watching the bats swoop over their heads to drink from the stream. Twice they heard the long, eerie screech of a barn owl. The sudden noise was so close it made them both jump. After half an hour Poppy had cramp in one foot and even Charlie the expert tracker was beginning to get restless.

"Five more minutes," she said softly. Charlie nodded and once more they settled down to wait.

Charlie was the first to hear a rustle in the undergrowth and he clutched Poppy's arm. The sound was coming from the far side of the river and they strained their eyes to see. Behind the undergrowth and interwoven branches was a ghostly shape which gradually began to take form as it drew closer. Charlie's grip on Poppy's arm grew tighter and she realised she was holding her breath as the shape finally emerged from the trees. Poppy felt the hairs on the back of her neck stand up.

It wasn't a puma or a jaguar. It was a dappled grey pony, which stopped and sniffed the air cautiously before stepping forward to drink from the river. The pony was bigger than Blaze and Flynn and was of a much finer build. He had dark grey points and a tail so long it brushed the floor. He drank thirstily, his coat briefly turning silver in the moonlight. Poppy gazed at the pony, wondering where he'd come from and how he'd ended up in their wood. She was surprised he couldn't hear her heart hammering.

She was so focussed on the pony that she didn't see Charlie reach into his pocket, take out his camera, point it and click. For a split second the flash lit the air and the pony half-reared in shock, whinnied and wheeled off into the trees.

Poppy rounded on her brother. "Charlie, you idiot! Look what you've done!"

"Sorry Poppy, I didn't mean to scare it away. I forgot about the flash." He looked so crestfallen she didn't have the heart to say any more.

"Anyway, we've seen loads of Dartmoor ponies since we moved here. Why are you so upset about this one running off?" he asked.

"That was no Dartmoor pony," replied Poppy, standing up to let the blood flow back into her cramped foot. "I don't know where he's come from or why he's living wild but I intend to find out."

CHAPTER 10

The next morning, Poppy was so convinced that the pony was a figment of her imagination that she'd gone into Charlie's bedroom, found his camera and checked that the photo he'd taken actually existed. After scrolling through various out-of-focus images of her and Caroline and a few of Chester, she came to the photograph she was looking for. Charlie had captured the pony half-rearing in the moonlight in the moment before he turned and fled. Although the image was fuzzy Poppy could make out his flared nostrils and brown eyes full of fear. The sight made her heart twist painfully.

"Where could he have come from?" she asked Scarlett later that morning, as the pair tacked up Flynn and Blaze before setting off on a gentle ride on the moor. Poppy loved hacking out. Flynn was such a gentleman that she overlooked his tendency to grab a mouthful of grass whenever he thought he could get away with it.

"I've no idea but I bet I can guess who does," Scarlett replied.

"Tory!" Poppy answered. She'd spent the morning wondering if the old woman knew more than she was letting on. Her evasiveness and the wistful way she'd looked into the wood suggested she might know something about the mysterious grey pony. Poppy was desperate to quiz Tory about him.

As luck would have it she didn't have to wait long. After weeks of sun the weather finally broke the next day and, faced with the unappealing prospect of a rainy Saturday afternoon at home entertaining an energetic Charlie, Caroline had suggested they go into Tavistock for a trip to the library followed by a cream tea.

"While you two are in the library, could I go and see Tory? I want to show her the photos Charlie took of Chester after I gave him that bath," Poppy asked, holding her breath while Caroline considered the request.

In Twickenham her stepmother never let the children out of her sight but she'd become much more relaxed since they'd moved to Devon. Poppy was eleven and about to start secondary school after all. She needed some independence.

"Good idea. I'll drop you off at Tory's flat and then we can meet in the cafe opposite the town hall at three o'clock. I've got her address here somewhere."

Caroline fished about in a drawer in the oak dresser until she found the scrap of paper she was looking for.

"Here it is. Right, shall we go? Charlie, have you got your library books?"

The windscreen wipers were going nineteen to the dozen as Caroline drew up outside the block of sheltered flats where Tory lived.

"Tory's flat is number twelve. Give her our love and we'll see you at three," Caroline said. Poppy pulled on her hood and made a run for the flats. As she splashed through puddles to the disabled ramp at the front of the building, the strident tones of a woman's voice made her start.

"Hello! Can I help you?" It sounded more like a threat than a question. The woman stuck her head out of the entrance door and looked at a rain-sodden Poppy with distaste, as if she was something the cat had dragged in. "I'm Mrs Parker and I'm the warden here. You're not one of those dreadful hoodies are you?" she said, peering closely at Poppy. She was, Poppy guessed, in her late fifties and had a helmet of tightly permed grey hair that didn't move when she looked Poppy up and down. She wore a heavy tweed skirt of a nondescript brown and a fawn-coloured twinset with an obligatory string of pearls. Unfortunately the lady-of-the-manor look was ruined by her pink, fluffy, rabbit-shaped slippers. Mrs Parker caught Poppy staring at her feet and the girl's perplexed expression seemed to antagonise her further.

"Well, do you have a tongue in that head of yours?" she asked sharply.

"I'm Poppy. I'm a friend of Tory's. Can you show me where her flat is, please?" Poppy attempted a winning smile.

"I might have known," Mrs Parker muttered, opening the door wide enough for Poppy to step inside. The warden's helmet of hair remained motionless as she turned and pointed along a dimly lit corridor.

"Down there, second door on the right. She's in - I can hear her television from here. Well, what are you waiting for - Christmas?" Mrs Parker asked rudely, as Poppy stood rooted to the spot. "And I don't want any trouble from either of you!" With that, she turned on the heel of her slippers and stalked off in the opposite direction.

Poppy pulled back her hood, sending raindrops scattering, and walked along the corridor, stopping when she saw a ceramic plaque painted with the number twelve and a pretty border of pink roses. She knocked softly and then with more force so Tory would hear her over the sound of the television. Her friend opened the door a crack and, seeing a bedraggled Poppy standing outside, opened it wide, a broad smile on her weather-beaten face.

"Poppy! What a lovely surprise. Come in, you look absolutely soaked. Sit down over here. You can tell me how Chester is while I make you a drink. I'm missing the old boy dreadfully. Did you meet Mrs Parker? See what I mean? She has me down as a trouble-maker, all because I've started organising a poker night in the residents' lounge every Friday. It's very popular but the old dragon doesn't approve, says it's lowering the tone. And it's not like it's strip poker! This place needs livening up a bit if you ask me."

Poppy sank gratefully into one of the two armchairs in Tory's front room and looked around her while Tory turned off the television and went into the kitchen to put the kettle on. Tory's lounge had a window overlooking a small courtyard. Doors led off to a galley kitchen, a tiny bedroom and an even smaller bathroom. There was a faint smell of toast. Poppy got the impression that more furniture than there was room for had been shoehorned into the flat. The two armchairs were covered in a busy floral fabric and each was draped in lace antimacassars. Against one of the magnolia walls was a glass-fronted dark wood cabinet filled with porcelain figurines. An old oak gate-leg table with barley twist legs stood between the two armchairs, its surface covered in framed photographs.

As Tory chatted away in the kitchen, Poppy stole a look at the pictures. One, a sepia portrait of a young couple looking seriously into the lens, must have been Tory and Douglas on their wedding day. There was a photo of the couple and a small girl aged about five standing in front of Riverdale. She must be Jo, the daughter Tory had fallen out with. Other pictures showed Tory's family through the passing of years and Poppy was beginning to lose interest when a photo half hidden at the back caught her eye. She reached out to have a closer look and what she saw made her stomach flip over. The photo showed a girl on a dappled grey pony being presented with a red rosette by a man in a hacking jacket. Peering closer, she could just make out the words Brambleton Horse Show around the edge of the rosette. As Tory shuffled slowly in with Poppy's tea she guiltily tried to put the photo back in its place but in her haste toppled over the two frames in front of it.

"I wondered if you'd notice that," said Tory, gently placing the mug on a small stool next to Poppy's armchair.

"It's the same pony I've seen in the wood, isn't it Tory? You know where he came from, don't you? Please tell me."

Tory picked up the photo and sat down heavily in the other chair. She looked at the girl and pony and her face sagged in sadness.

"Yes, I do know where the pony came from, pet. But it's a long story with no happy ending. Are you really sure you want to know?"

CHAPTER 11

"I used to be a bit of a rider myself in my day," Tory began, settling herself into her armchair as the rain pounded against the window.

"You didn't tell me that," said Poppy, taking a sip of the milky tea, feeling its warmth spread through her. She held the mug in both hands as Tory smiled.

"Nothing major but I used to compete in local shows and hunter trials. A couple of times I even entered the showjumping classes at the Devon County Show on my mare Hopscotch. She was a chestnut thoroughbred, a beautiful horse, so willing and nice-natured. You would have loved her. When our daughter was born I assumed she would be as pony-mad as I'd been but Jo suffered badly from asthma and being around horses often brought on an attack. Perhaps because of this she was always nervous around them and, of course, they picked up on it. It wasn't a happy combination.

"Then, 18 years ago, Jo's daughter Caitlyn was born. Almost from the time she could walk Caitlyn lived and breathed horses and would pester her mum into bringing her to Riverdale to spend time with Hopscotch and Chester. Hopscotch was virtually retired by then but I used to put Caitlyn up on her and take them both onto the moors on the leading rein for hours at a time. Cait looked like a pea on a drum but she loved it.

"When she was about six I was given Sparky, a roan Dartmoor pony, on loan as a companion for Hopscotch and Chester and, of course, he soon became Caitlyn's pony. Jo wasn't best pleased but Caitlyn adored him and the two of them joined the pony club and competed in gymkhanas and local horse shows."

Poppy tried not to feel envious of Caitlyn, who'd had the kind of pony-filled childhood she'd always dreamed of.

"Eventually Caitlyn grew too big for Sparky. Jo didn't want her to have a bigger pony and was keen for her to give up riding altogether to concentrate on her schoolwork, but I disagreed. Cait was a really instinctive, gutsy rider and I felt sure that with the right pony she could compete at a county level, if not higher.

"Then I heard about a shipment of ponies that had come over from Ireland and were being sold at the next horse sale at Newton Abbot. I drove over there in my horsebox one April afternoon thinking it was worth a try."

"How long ago was that?" Poppy asked, intrigued.

"Let me think. It must have been six years ago now. Caitlyn was 12 at the time. I didn't tell her or her mother what I was doing. I didn't want to get Cait's hopes up and I knew Jo would try to talk me out of it. So I turned up at the sale and there was the usual mix of coloured colts and mares with foals at foot with the odd riding pony thrown in. The Irish ponies were listed last. They were all nice-looking ponies, mainly Connemaras that had been backed but needed bringing on.

"But the last pony really caught my eye. He was a 14.2hh dappled grey with a handsome face and lovely conformation. He was very nervous and skittered around the ring shying at everything. But he had the kindest eyes. I had a gut feeling he was the right pony for Caitlyn."

Poppy knew the answer but she asked anyway. "Did you buy him?"

"Yes. I got him for a song because it was the end of the day and I think people were worried he was a bit flighty. Jo was so cross she wouldn't speak to me for a couple of days but Caitlyn was on cloud nine. She fell in love with him in an instant. And that's what we called him - Cloud Nine, or Cloud for short."

"What was he like?" asked Poppy.

"He was gentle with me and Cait but he was a different pony around men. When the farrier came to shoe him he went berserk in his stable and it took over an hour for him to calm down. I'm sure he must have been treated roughly at some stage. But he and Cait clicked straight away. We spent the first few weeks gaining his confidence, just grooming him, tacking him up and taking him out for hours on long reins. All the handling paid off and when Caitlyn did finally ride him he went like a dream.

"Soon they were jumping at local shows and winning their classes easily. Cloud would do anything for Caitlyn. They trusted each other completely. She was desperate to follow in my footsteps and compete in a hunter trial. Her mum was dead set against it. She said it was too dangerous but I talked her around."

Tory picked up the photograph of the girl and her pony again as if drawing strength for the final part of her story. "We found a novice hunter trial for her in Widecombe. She was so excited she and Cloud practised for hours jumping fallen trees and ditches on the moors. After weeks of dry weather the day of the competition was as wet as today." Tory looked at the window where the rain was still beating a steady drum against the glass.

"The course was as slippery as a skid pan. Jo pleaded with Caitlyn not to compete but I convinced her they would both be fine, that Cloud had studs in his shoes, he was a really careful jumper and that he'd look after her."

Poppy could hardly bear to hear what happened next.

"They set off well and Cloud was jumping out of his skin." Tory gave a half sob before carrying on. "Every hunter trial has its bogey fence and this one was a drop fence followed by a ditch three quarters of the way around the course."

Poppy had seen drop fences at Badminton and Burghley. Often a log or brush fence, they looked straightforward but had a steep drop on the other side so horse and rider landed on a lower level than the one they'd taken off from.

"The bank on the other side of the fence had been completely churned up and those horses that hadn't refused were slipping down it," remembered Tory. She and Jo had been standing close to the fence as Cait and Cloud galloped towards it. Tory remembered the pony's ears flick back as he hesitated for a second before taking off.

"I don't know what happened next, no-one really did. Whether he had been spooked by something in the crowd or by the height of the drop I don't know, but Cloud suddenly twisted in mid-air. As he landed he lost his footing and somersaulted over, throwing Cait underneath him."

Five years later the scene was still imprinted on Tory's memory as if it had happened that morning. Cloud had struggled to his feet and given an almighty shake. Below him Cait was lying motionless on the ground. Jo had screamed and together they had run over, Tory repeating under her breath, 'She's just winded herself, she's just winded, she'll sit up in a minute.'

But thirteen-year-old Caitlyn never did sit up. Within minutes an ambulance, its blue lights flashing and its sirens screaming, arrived and a screen was erected around the young rider, shielding her from the crowds as the paramedics carried her still body onto the ambulance and away.

By now the tears were streaming down Tory's lined cheeks. "Her death was all my fault. I should never have encouraged Cait to enter the competition. If it wasn't for me she'd still be here. She would have been eighteen by now. She had her whole life ahead of her and because of me she never even reached her fourteenth birthday.

"Jo blamed me for Cait's death and I don't blame her. She's not spoken to me since. I would do anything to turn back the clock, Poppy. I lost a daughter and a granddaughter that day."

"What happened to Cloud?" Poppy asked quietly.

"One of the course officials took him back to the lorry and by the time I got back he was shivering with cold or exhaustion - or both. You probably think I'm being sentimental when I tell you that his heart was broken that day. I think he knew what had happened. We both felt responsible for Caitlyn's death."

Tory explained how she had taken Cloud back to Riverdale but that the pony's spirit had been destroyed. She recalled how, in a fug of misery, she had sold him to a pugnacious man called George Blackstone in the hope that it would appease Jo.

Blackstone, who farmed the far side of the valley, was a member of the local hunt and prided himself on his horsemanship skills. But he wasn't a kind man and Tory told Poppy how she had watched, powerless, as Cloud sank into deeper despair. The pony didn't even have the energy to fight back as Blackstone, realising he'd been sold a dud, took his frustration out on him.

"Selling Cloud to Blackstone was a terrible mistake, I quickly realised that," said Tory. "I knew I had to do something - I owed it to Cloud. I tried to buy him back several times but Blackstone flatly refused - he was convinced he could, as he put it, 'knock some sense into the pony'."

Poppy suspected that Cloud must have been the colt the two old farmhands had been talking about in the post office the day Caroline had popped in for stamps. "How did Cloud end up living wild?" she asked Tory, not imagining that Blackstone would have ever set him free.

For the first time since she'd begun her story the old woman looked at Poppy with something resembling a glint in her eye. "Let's just say he was liberated one night."

The loud chimes of the antique clock on Tory's mantlepiece made Poppy jump and she realised with surprise that it was three o'clock.

"Oh no! I'm supposed to be meeting Caroline and Charlie at three. I'd better go or I'll be really late." She looked at Tory. "Thank-you for telling me about Caitlyn and Cloud. I'm sure Charlie and I have seen Cloud drinking from the stream in the wood next to Riverdale although he galloped off as soon as he saw us."

"I'm glad. I worry about him. And there's nothing I can do to help him stuck here."

Poppy thought again of the conversation Caroline had overheard in the post office. Something about the annual drift. But she didn't have time to think about it now. "I'm going to have to go, Tory. But please come and see me and Chester soon. I need to know if there's anything I can do to help Cloud."

Poppy felt a rush of affection for the old woman and she reached over and gave her a hug. Tory beamed, although her eyes had grown misty again. "You're a lovely girl, Poppy, and you remind me so much of Caitlyn. Now, off you go before Caroline starts worrying you've been kidnapped by aliens, and watch out for Nosy Parker in the hallway - the interfering old bat's probably listening at the door."

CHAPTER 12

The next morning it was still raining and Caroline suggested that Poppy invite Scarlett over for lunch. Poppy was upstairs daydreaming about Cloud when she heard her friend at the back door and by the time she had jumped down the stairs, two at a time, Scarlett was deep in conversation with Caroline in the kitchen. They were talking about the girls' new school and Scarlett was regaling Caroline with outrageous stories about the children from her primary school who would be in their year. Caroline had seemed down in the dumps recently but her face was animated as she listened to Scarlett's colourful descriptions of her former classmates and she laughed out loud as Scarlett told a story about a particularly obnoxious boy called Darren who had once fed chalk dust to the class goldfish. I never make her laugh like that, thought Poppy despondently, as she pasted a smile to her face and walked in to join them.

"Do you two want to give me a hand with the vegetables?" Caroline asked. The three of them spent the next half an hour at the kitchen table shelling peas, slicing runner beans and discussing the pros and cons of their new burgundy and navy school uniform. Poppy's was hanging up in her wardrobe, a glaring reminder that the summer holiday was almost over.

After lunch Poppy finally managed to get Scarlett on her own when the two of them went to muck out Chester's stable. She was bursting to recount the previous day's conversation with Tory.

"That explains everything. No wonder Tory and her daughter fell out. Poor Tory, she must have been heart-broken. I suppose I would only have been about five at the time, otherwise I would have remembered it," said Scarlett. "One thing that puzzles me though," she continued. "How did Cloud avoid being rounded up with all the Dartmoor ponies in the drift every year?"

"I'm pretty sure Tory used to hide him in Chester's stable while the drift was on," said Poppy, who'd thought of little else all night. "Which means Cloud must still trust her, despite everything."

"But why hide him? Why didn't she just come clean and give him a permanent home where he'd be safe and cared for?" asked Scarlett, puzzled.

"Because George Blackstone still owns him, I suppose. According to Tory he wouldn't sell Cloud back to her after Caitlyn died, even though she pleaded with him to. Perhaps he still thinks he can make a competition pony out of Cloud."

Scarlett knew the belligerent farmer of old, and suspected that he'd refused to sell the pony back to Tory out of sheer pig-headedness, but she kept the thought to herself.

"What about this year though, Scarlett?" wailed Poppy. "What's going to happen to Cloud now Tory's in Tavistock? He'll be rounded up and sent back to George Blackstone who'll pick up where he left off five years ago, trying to 'beat some sense into him'. I can't let that happen."

"Don't panic. We just need to come up with a plan. I'll find out when the drift is - my dad'll know - and you need to speak to Tory again and tell her we need to know how she managed to catch Cloud."

"Who's Cloud?" piped up a voice from the stable door and Poppy's heart sank right to the bottom of her borrowed jodhpur boots. Who knew how much of the conversation Charlie had heard.

"No-one for you to worry about, little brother. Come on Scarlett, we're done here. Why don't you go inside and dry off while I go and catch Chester." She grabbed the donkey's headcollar from its peg and headed for Chester's paddock, irritated to see that Charlie was following her.

"Is Cloud the white pony we saw by the stream?" he asked, running to keep up with her as she strode across the field, her head bent against the driving rain.

"None of your business. And anyway, you never call a horse white, it's always grey," she said, knowing she was splitting hairs but hoping it would put him off the scent. No such luck.

"It is my business. And if you don't tell me I'll tell Mum about the pony and it'll be her business too," he replied, smiling evilly at his sister.

Poppy knew she had lost. Charlie was as tenacious as a fox terrier. She stopped and turned to face her brother, sighing loudly. "Alright, I will tell you but not now. Tonight, I promise. But you've got to give me your word that you won't breathe a whisper of it to anyone, especially Caroline. And I mean that, OK?"

She tried to look as menacing as she could but Charlie wasn't exactly quaking in his wellies. Instead, while nodding vigorously, he was trying hard to suppress a jubilant smile. Typical, she thought, as she caught Chester and led him to the shelter of his newly mucked-out stable. She would now need to baby-sit Charlie as they tried to rescue Cloud from the drift. As if she didn't have enough to worry about.

Satisfied he wouldn't be missing out on any excitement, Charlie disappeared back indoors. Poppy tied Chester up inside the stable and began rubbing him down with an old towel.

"Did you help Tory look after Cloud?" she murmured to the old donkey. He turned and looked at her with his clear brown eyes and Poppy got the sense that he had been very much involved in the annual rescue operation. She remembered back to their first night at Riverdale when she'd heard a horse's lonely whinny and Chester had returned the call. The two had been stablemates for almost a year before Caitlyn's death. As she scratched the donkey's ears absentmindedly she realised he probably held the key to saving Cloud from the drift and a life of certain misery with George Blackstone.

The rain was still beating its relentless tattoo against the windows of Riverdale that evening as Poppy, Charlie and Caroline settled down after dinner to watch the six o'clock news. Her dad was giving a live broadcast from the Middle East.

"When is Dad coming home?" asked Poppy, who was cheered to see her leather friendship bracelet peeking out from his right cuff.

"We were hoping he'd be back before you both started school but he texted this afternoon to say he might have to do another couple of weeks," said Caroline, her eyes fixed on the television screen. After his report the presenter turned to a story about a reported sighting of a puma-type animal in the Peak District.

"See!" shouted Charlie, bouncing up and down on the sofa. "There are big cats in the wild. It's not just me who thinks so."

"I'll read Charlie his story tonight if you like," Poppy offered a grateful Caroline, who had purple shadows under her eyes.

"That would be brilliant, thanks Poppy. Make sure

he cleans his teeth and washes his face. You know how allergic he is to soap."

"Will do. Come on Charlie, let's get you to bed. What do you fancy tonight - The Lion, The Witch and The Wardrobe or Spongebob Squarepants?"

"Spongebob, of course!" replied the six-year-old, following his sister out of the room.

Fifteen minutes later Charlie's face had been scrubbed clean, his teeth had been brushed and he was sitting in bed sucking his thumb, a long-held habit only the family were ever allowed to witness. He took his thumb out briefly to ask, "Now will you tell me about Cloud?"

Poppy gave him an edited version of the pony's history and how he had come to be roaming wild on the moors. "Now we need to work out how to keep him safe from this year's drift, otherwise Blackstone will get his hands on him again and either sell him or, even worse, keep him."

"Couldn't you just buy him?" asked Charlie, with all the logic of a six-year-old.

"I've got about two pounds fifty in my piggy bank, Charlie. I spent all my money on Chester's new grooming kit," she reminded him.

"We need to find a way to capture him then, don't we?" He went quiet, his thumb firmly in, as he pondered the challenge. "I know!" he said, sitting up suddenly. "I can creep up on him upwind, and when I'm close enough I'll spit a sleeping dart through a straw into his bottom. You can get a headcollar on him while he's knocked out."

Poppy's raised eyebrows were enough to tell Charlie it wasn't going to happen.

"Alright then, we'll dig a massive pit, cover it with branches and put a bucket of Chester's pony nuts in the middle. Then when Cloud comes over for a nibble, he'll drop down into the pit."

Poppy tutted. "There's a saying Dad uses sometimes. Softly, softly, catchee monkey."

Charlie looked baffled. "But we want to catch a pony, not a monkey."

"You twit! It means I need to be patient if I stand any chance of catching Cloud. He's lost all faith in humans - apart from Tory - so I'm going to have to gain his trust and that could take ages."

"Please let me help you, Poppy. I promise I'll do whatever you say, and my tracking skills might come in useful." Poppy sincerely doubted it, but she had a feeling Charlie meant what he said, and it might be useful to have an extra pair of hands if Scarlett wasn't around.

"OK then. But you must give me your word you won't tell Caroline," she reiterated. She knelt down in front of his bookcase, tracing her fingers along the book spines until she came to Spongebob Squarepants.

"Why don't you ever call her mum?" said a small voice from the bed.

"Because she's not my mum and never will be." Poppy glanced at her half-brother, still sucking his thumb and looking at her solemnly with Caroline's big blue eyes.

"But your mum's dead so she's the only one you've got. You don't even seem to like her very much most of the time."

"You're too young to understand," said Poppy, neatly side-stepping the question. "Come on, shall we see what's happening in Bikini Bottom?"

CHAPTER 13

Scarlett fulfilled her promise to find out about the drift and put Poppy in the picture the next morning as they groomed and tacked up Flynn and Blaze.

"Every autumn all the Dartmoor ponies are rounded up so their owners can check them over to make sure they are healthy," she explained. "Foals born the previous spring are separated from their mothers and the foals are sold at market. So are any ponies that look like they might not survive another winter on Dartmoor. The hardiest ponies are returned to the moor to breed."

"How do they round the ponies up?" Poppy asked, fascinated.

"They use local people on quad bikes, horseback and on foot. It's quite a task because sometimes as many as three thousand ponies need to be rounded up, Dad said."

"No wonder Tory decided to hide Cloud. He'd have been completely traumatised and would have stuck out like a sore thumb among all those Dartmoor ponies. He's at least a couple of hands higher," said Poppy.

"When are you next seeing Tory?" Scarlett asked.

"Tomorrow. Caroline has invited her to tea. I can't wait to ask her how she managed to catch Cloud every year."

"Well, Dad says this year's drift is less than a month away, which doesn't give us very long."

When Poppy arrived home after her ride she let herself in through the back door and went in search of a carrot for Chester. She could hear Caroline talking on the phone in the lounge and, without thinking, inched closer to the open door.

"I just feel as if there's this huge black weight bringing me down. And I'm so tired all the time, Lizzie. I can hardly get out of bed in the morning and by nine o'clock in the evening I'm asleep on the sofa. That's not like me."

Lizzie was Caroline's older sister. A secondary school teacher in Bromley with two teenage sons, she was straight-talking but a lot of fun. Although weeks could go by without them seeing each other, the two sisters were close and spoke every couple of days on the phone.

Poppy held her breath as Caroline listened to Lizzie's reply.

"I thought moving to Devon would be a new start. Don't get me wrong, Lizzie, I love the house and Poppy and Charlie adore it here, it's been so good for them both, but I'm lonely. I miss Mike, I miss you and I miss my friends. I've started talking to the sheep, for goodness sake!" But her attempt at a laugh turned into a sniff.

Poppy could imagine Lizzie in the untidy kitchen of her town house in Bromley 250 miles away. She'd be sitting on the small sofa that looked out onto her immaculately-kept garden. Gardening was one of Lizzie's passions. Housework was absolutely not.

"Charlie's convinced there's a big cat living wild on the moors and is constantly dreaming up madcap schemes to find it and Poppy spends all her time with Scarlett - the girl from the farm next door I told you about?"

Poppy stiffened at the sound of her name.

"No, nothing's changed. I thought leaving Twickenham might be a clean break for us all but she's still so prickly with me. Whatever I do or say seems to be the wrong thing. It's like she's still punishing me for Isobel's death, after all these years."

There was silence again as Caroline listened to her sister's reply.

"I know, I will. And I promise I'll go and see the doctor if I still don't feel any better in a couple of weeks. Anyway, I'd better make a start on dinner. Thanks for listening to my woes and give my love to Stuart and the boys. Bye Lizzie."

Poppy was busying herself by the vegetable rack rooting among the potatoes and onions for a carrot by the time Caroline came into the kitchen. She was wearing yesterday's rumpled clothes and her hair, usually so shiny, needed a wash.

"Hello Poppy, did you have a good ride? How was Flynn today - did he go well for you?" Caroline asked brightly, the light tone of her voice contradicting the weary sag in her shoulders as she sat down at the kitchen table. Perversely her stepmother's well-intentioned enquiries irked Poppy, who located two good-sized carrots and straightened up.

"What's this - twenty questions?" The words came out before she could stop herself. Even to her own ears she sounded surly.

"Sorry sweetheart - I was only asking. What do you fancy for dinner? I've only got mince so it'll have to be spaghetti bolognese or cottage pie but you can choose."

"Um, bolognese, I guess. I'm going out to groom Chester."

Poppy heard Caroline sigh as she flung the back door shut behind her. As she stomped out to Chester's stable she thought about the conversation she'd overheard. How dare Caroline call her prickly? She missed her mum, that was all, and the sooner Caroline realised she could never replace Isobel the better, as far as she was concerned. Her stepmother was always so annoyingly cheerful and capable it was difficult to believe she was lonely and maybe even a bit depressed. Poppy dismissed the thought. She was just exaggerating, knowing she'd get a sympathetic reaction from her sister. A nagging feeling told her Caroline wasn't the type to go fishing for sympathy but she ignored it, gave Chester a gentle pat on the rump and started brushing the burrs from his tail, all thoughts of her stepmother forgotten.

Caroline made an extra effort for Tory the following day. She baked a chocolate cake - Charlie's favourite, Poppy thought sourly - and made a quiche which she planned to serve with lettuce and tomatoes from the garden. Tory caught the bus to the end of the drive and was delighted to see a small welcoming committee made up of Caroline, Poppy and Charlie waiting to help her up to the house.

Poppy and Caroline took an arm each and as they walked Tory's head tracked back and forth, taking in the paddocks, the wood and the tor, which was basked in sunshine.

"I know it's only been a few weeks but it feels grand to be back," said Tory, as they finally made it to the front door and Caroline helped her off with her coat.

"Charlie and I have a surprise for you," Poppy said. "Sit here and close your eyes." She motioned to a wrought iron bench in front of the house. "Come on, Charlie."

The two children had spent the morning giving Chester the grooming of his life. Poppy had weaved red ribbons into his thick mane and tail and Charlie had brushed his hooves with oil until they glistened. Charlie proudly led the donkey round to the front of the house. "You can open your eyes now!"

"Oh my, don't you look handsome!" Tory told Chester, ferreting around in her handbag for some Polos. The donkey accepted one graciously.

"Thank you Poppy and Charlie, what a lovely surprise. Chester looks so well, you've obviously been looking after him beautifully."

Poppy smiled and Charlie gave a little bow. "All part of the Riverdale service, madam," he said with a grin.

For the rest of the day the house buzzed. Poppy realised how quiet it had been over the past few weeks with Caroline so listless. Even Charlie, naturally so exuberant, had been less boisterous than usual, perhaps picking up on his mum's downcast mood. But Tory cheered everyone up. Despite being 'absolutely ancient' as she described herself, she had an incorrigible sense of fun and made them laugh with tales of colourful local characters and recollections of the many happy years she and her husband, Douglas, had spent living at Riverdale.

Later Tory and Poppy sat on the bench at the front of the house, enjoying a cup of tea and a slice of cake as they caught the last rays of the sun. Breaking the companionable silence Tory said, "I've been having a long chat with Caroline this afternoon."

The stone wall behind them felt warm to the touch

and there was a background hum of bees as they buzzed lazily around two lavender-filled terracotta pots on either side of the bench. "She seems very low. Nothing like the woman I met the day you all moved in." Tory took a sip from her mug and looked out across the valley.

Poppy kicked her heels against the ground and shrugged. "She's probably just a bit lonely. Missing Dad and her friends in London, I expect."

"No, I think it's more than that." Tory looked Poppy in the eye. "I remember when I was your age. I thought the world revolved around me. All children do, I suppose it's a survival instinct. Teenagers are probably the most self-absorbed of the lot, although some old people can be just as selfish - I suppose we all come full circle in the end," she mused.

With a little shake of her head she carried on. "Of course, once you have children that all changes. Women like Caroline think of everyone else first, they have to be totally selfless. I'm sure your mum was the same."

Poppy nodded. In the years since her death Isobel had taken on the status of a saint in Poppy's eyes. She had subconsciously provided Caroline with an impossible act to follow.

"Native Americans have a saying - don't judge a man until you have walked a mile in his shoes," Tory continued.

Poppy wondered where the conversation was heading. She had a sneaking suspicion she wasn't going to like it.

"Have you ever walked in Caroline's shoes?" Tory asked, and Poppy pictured herself staggering down the bumpy Riverdale drive in Caroline's favourite red killer heels. Supressing the image she shook her head.

"What I'm trying to say," persevered Tory, "in a long and convoluted way, is this. I know you miss your mum and always will, but have you ever stopped to think about Caroline and how she is feeling?"

"Why do people keep on at me about Caroline? First Scarlett, then Charlie and now you. I thought you were on my side!"

"I am, pet. I'm just trying to make things better for everyone. I hate to think of Riverdale as an unhappy house." Tory took a deep breath in a nothing ventured, nothing gained kind of way and changed tack. "Caroline was telling me today about Isobel's accident. It must have been so hard for you when she died."

Poppy nodded. She knew Tory understood what it was like to lose someone you loved. But the old woman's next comment hit her in the solar plexus. "I may be wrong but I get the feeling you blame Caroline for Isobel's death."

"That's not true! Dad didn't even meet Caroline until after Mum died. The only person I blame is me! Mum was run over because I ran back into the road, didn't Caroline tell you that?" Poppy's eyes flashed dangerously.

"She told me it was an accident, pet, and that if

anyone was to blame it was the driver who was going too fast on a busy road so near a school."

Poppy continued kicking the ground viciously as Tory ploughed on. "Blaming yourself is no good - the guilt will just eat you up. You've got to accept it wasn't your fault and move on, Poppy."

"You sound like one of those awful bereavement counsellors Dad made me see after Mum died! Pathetic do-gooders who couldn't do any good because they couldn't turn back the clock, could they?"

"I know, pet, no-one can turn back the clock. But you should know that Caroline feels…"

Poppy never did find out how her stepmother felt as before Tory could finish she had stalked off to her bedroom, banging the door shut as ferociously as she dared and refusing to come down to say goodbye when Tory's nephew turned up half an hour later to take her home.

That night Poppy dreamt about the accident. Her four-year-old self held Ears in one hand and the other was clasped firmly in her mum's. But her hand felt different and when she looked down at their shadows her mum's was tall and willowy, not small and slim. They crossed the road, heading for home, and reached the pavement on the other side. She realised she'd dropped the rabbit, slipped out of her mum's grip and ran back into the road. But when she looked up, Ears dangling from her fist, the face staring back at her, white with terror, wasn't Isobel's. It was

Caroline's.

"Mummy!" shouted four-year-old Poppy in the dream, and Caroline took two steps forward and swept her into her arms and to safety. They both spun around to look as the speeding car flashed past. Poppy pressed her face into Caroline's neck, breathing in the familiar scent. She felt safe and loved. Caroline murmured into her hair, "Oh Poppy, my darling girl. Everything will be alright. I promise."

CHAPTER 14

"So, basically, you ran off in a strop without asking Tory anything about Cloud?" demanded Scarlett the next afternoon. Poppy was sitting, cross-legged, on the red and royal blue rug on her bedroom floor. Scarlett was sprawled on her bed, leafing through old editions of Poppy's pony magazines. Charlie, who had been allowed in under the strict conditions that he only spoke when spoken to and didn't breathe a word of their conversation to Caroline, was sitting on the wicker chair by the window playing on his DS. Magpie lay curled in a ball on the carpet, his substantial stomach illuminated by a shaft of sunlight.

"I know. I was an idiot, you don't have to tell me," groaned Poppy, who had felt slightly out of kilter since she'd woken up, the previous night's dream refusing to fade from her mind's eye. "The trouble is

I'm not sure when I'll next get a chance to talk to Tory. She probably won't even want to see me after the way I stormed off yesterday. We're never going to find out how she managed to catch Cloud."

Scarlett had stopped listening. Her eye had been caught by an article in one of the magazines. "Look at this! How to be a Horse Whisperer," she read. "It's a whole feature on gaining the confidence of even the most nervous of horses." Poppy jumped up and joined her on the bed and they pored over the article.

"What does it say then?" asked Charlie, glancing up from his DS. Magpie lifted his black and white face and looked at the two girls with interest.

"That a horse won't trust you until he has confidence in you. That you've got to think about how he feels and the things he fears. Look, there are lots of tips...don't make eye contact, turn your back to him so he gets curious and seeks your attention, talk or sing to him so he gets used to your voice. If he heard me singing he'd run for the hills. Mum says I'm tone deaf," said Scarlett gloomily.

"What you need is some direct action. You're not going to get Cloud to trust you by sitting in your bedroom talking about it," said Charlie, ever the pragmatist.

"But we go to Granny's tomorrow! We won't be back until the day before term starts," moaned Scarlett, who was not looking forward to the family's annual pilgrimage to her grandparents' draughty farmhouse in Wiltshire.

"Sorry Scarlett, but for once Charlie is right. I need to start if we stand any chance of catching Cloud before the drift. I'll text you to let you know how we're getting on. You'll be back before you know it."

Scarlett had been summoned home for tea and Poppy and Charlie walked with her back to the farm, taking a handful of carrots with them for Flynn and Blaze. Scarlett was subdued and for once it was down to Poppy to keep the conversation going.

"You know Scar, you won't miss anything. It's probably going to take weeks to get anywhere near Cloud, let alone catch him," she told her glum-faced friend.

"I know. It's just that I hate going to Granny's. I miss Blaze heaps when we're away and now I won't be able to help you with Cloud. It's so unfair!"

Poppy nodded sympathetically and gave Scarlett a brief hug. "I'll text, I promise," she said. "Come on, Charlie. We'd better get going."

"You'll need someone to go with you though, won't you?" said her brother, his blue eyes turned hopefully towards hers as they walked across the sheep field to Riverdale.

Poppy sighed. "I suppose so. But you know the rules, little brother."

"Yes, the rules. No talking, no moving, no making any noise, no breathing. I know, I'll play dead, then I'm bound to stay out of trouble."

"Ha ha, very funny. Shall we go tonight?" She paused. "What should we tell Caroline?"

"Leave that to me," replied Charlie, who had the satisfied look of a man with a plan.

"Mum?" he said, tracking Caroline down in the kitchen where she was standing by the sink looking blankly out of the window. Poppy found her utter stillness unnerving but as Caroline turned to face them her face cleared and she smiled.

"Oh, there you are, you two. What have you been doing?"

"That's what I wanted to tell you. We've been reading about badgers," Charlie said, producing a book on British wildlife from behind his back with a flourish. "We've been looking at their habitat and how to spot signs that they have a sett nearby. What badger poo looks like and stuff like that," he explained earnestly, his blue eyes fixed on Caroline's. "We were wondering if we could go out into the woods after tea and see if we can find any. Badgers, that is, not badger poo. Although, of course, if you find the poo you'll find the badgers."

"Yes, I get the picture," laughed Caroline. She thought for a moment. "Yes, I don't see why not, as long as you take your phone Poppy, you don't go too far and you're back before it gets dark."

Poppy looked at her brother with a mixture of astonishment and admiration. Six years old and totally unfazed at fabricating stories. How did he manage it?

They set off just after six o'clock, armed with binoculars, phone, camera and Charlie's wildlife book.

"Hold on, I've just remembered something," said

Poppy. She darted into the tackroom next to Chester's stable, emerging seconds later with a scoop of pony nuts in a bucket. "I'm sure Chester won't mind. They are for his friend, after all," she whispered.

"Shall we go to the little beach where we saw him before?" asked Charlie, who was bouncing along beside his sister. There was nothing Charlie loved more than direct action.

"Yes, I think that's probably as good a place as any," Poppy answered and they crossed the field in front of the house, climbed the fence and disappeared into the wood.

Twenty minutes later they arrived at the clearing. Recent rain had turned the meandering stream into a fast-flowing river, which whooshed noisily past them.

"Let's put the bucket of nuts on the beach, go and hide behind that tree again and see if he comes," said Poppy, feeling sick with nerves.

They crouched down behind the tree and waited. It was a windy evening and the branches sighed and creaked around them. The light was beginning to fade and as the sun set to the west it cast long shadows that rippled and danced across the woodland floor. Charlie grew fidgety. Poppy nudged him to be still.

"Sorry," he whispered. "But I need the toilet."

She sighed loudly and stood up. "Great. Look, go over there behind that bush. And try and be quiet about it, will you?"

When Charlie returned, a leaf sticking out of his

hair, he sat down and started silently flicking through his book on wildlife. Every now and then he stopped, licked the pad of his index finger and held it up to the wind, nodding sagely. Poppy didn't know whether to hug him or throttle him. Instead she fixed her eyes on the line of trees in front of them and stared so hard that the leaves dissolved into a blur of green. She checked the time on the glowing face of her phone.

It was just as she was beginning to lose hope of Cloud ever turning up when there was a crackle in the branches and a sliver of silver through the leaves. Poppy felt her heart pounding. Even Charlie had let his book fall to his lap and was staring intently ahead.

They both watched breathlessly as Cloud poked his nose out of the trees. He sniffed the air, looking this way and that. Satisfied there was nothing to harm him he stepped slowly out into the clearing. Poppy and Charlie looked at each other and smiled. Poppy held her finger to her lips and Charlie nodded. He was determined not to do anything that might scare the pony this time.

Cloud was thinner than Poppy remembered and his coat looked dull. As he walked forwards, stopping every few paces to sniff the air, she saw he wasn't putting his full weight on his near hind leg. He hobbled over to the bucket, his neck stretched and his nostrils flared as he sniffed it. He was poised for flight and Poppy's heart was racing. Perhaps the smell of the pony nuts was too much to bear, perhaps he smelt the lingering scent of his old friend Chester, but after a few moments he began to eat noisily until the last nut had gone before taking another few uneven steps forward and drinking from the river.

The branches behind the two watching children rustled and Cloud looked up. He gave a start when he saw two pairs of eyes staring back at him from the other side of the river and Poppy immediately lowered her eyes, motioning Charlie to do the same. She held her breath, expecting him to turn on a sixpence and flee, but the pony stood watching them warily for a minute or two before limping slowly back off into the woods.

"I'm worried about him. He was lame, did you notice? And did you see how thin he looked?" Poppy asked her brother as they trudged back home through the dusk.

"At least he didn't run away as soon as he saw us, like he did before. So that's good, isn't it?" countered Charlie.

It was a start, thought Poppy as she settled down to sleep that night, the dead weight of a gently snoring Magpie pinning her feet down. But they still had a long way to go.

CHAPTER 15

The following day Caroline drove Poppy and Charlie into Plymouth to buy school shoes, rucksacks, pens and pencil cases, yet more reminders that their holiday was almost over. Poppy had visited her new high school briefly during their first week in Devon and had left feeling overwhelmed at the size of both the school and the students. They had been shown around by the head boy, Jordan White. Jordan was so long and lanky he looked as if he'd been stretched on a rack in some medieval torture chamber. Charlie had spent the entire morning staring with interest at an angry cluster of spots on his chin. Poppy had squirmed with embarrassment when the puzzled six-year-old had asked the sixthformer, 'Isn't Jordan a girl's name?'

She wondered how on earth she'd ever manage to

find her way around the countless corridors and classrooms with their unfamiliar odour of sweaty trainers and school dinners. She was beyond glad that Scarlett would be starting with her.

As they drove home across the moors, Poppy noticed for the first time that the trees were beginning to turn from vivid green to ochre. It wouldn't be long before the swallows disappeared and autumn arrived in their place. She thought of Cloud, facing the harsh Dartmoor winter not only lame but underweight, unlike the round, hardy Dartmoor ponies, whose coats were becoming thicker as the days grew shorter.

"So, are you two planning to go badger-watching this evening?" Caroline asked, as they crunched up the drive to home.

"Oh, yes please Mum." Charlie cast a sidelong look at his sister. "We found a hole in the roots of a tree that looked like it might be the entrance to a sett but even though we looked and looked we couldn't find any fresh poo, so it must be an old one."

"At least it shows there must be badgers about. It's just a case of tracking them down," said Poppy, who felt that Charlie's apparent interest in badger-watching was the perfect cover to see Cloud. When Charlie asked for something Caroline rarely said no.

That evening they ventured out to the wood an hour before dusk, Charlie taking two steps to Poppy's one as she strode purposefully across the field.

"I think we'll put the bucket in the same place, but tonight we'll sit on the tree instead of hiding behind it. We need him to start getting used to us," Poppy told her brother.

"Cool. I've brought some pictures I've drawn of some panther paw prints so we can look for them as well," Charlie produced a crumpled sheet of paper from deep inside the pocket of his shorts.

"You're not still on about that are you? We haven't even seen a badger in the woods, let alone a big cat." Seeing the indignant look on her brother's face Poppy decided there was no point antagonising him. "OK, on the way there and back we'll keep an eye out for paw prints, but while we're waiting for Cloud we need to be quiet and still. We can't afford to scare him."

Charlie dipped his head in assent. Soon they reached the bend in the river and Poppy placed the bucket on the small beach. This time she'd added a scoop of soaked sugar beet to the pony nuts to give Cloud extra energy. To her surprise they only had to wait for ten minutes before the pony ventured out into the open. He headed for the food and wolfed it down, only looking up once he had licked the bucket clean. Keeping her voice low and reassuring Poppy began talking to him. She felt self-conscious at first but Cloud pricked his grey ears and watched her without moving. So she prattled on until her steady monologue became part of the familiar noises of the wood.

After what seemed like hours but was probably only minutes Cloud lowered his head and drank from the river. He gave them one last look, then, with a swish of his tail, turned and hobbled off. Poppy looked at Charlie, her green eyes shining. "He's getting used to us, isn't he? He watched us for ages without moving. He knows we want to help him, I'm sure of it!"

But Charlie had more pressing matters on his mind. "Yes, it's brilliant, Poppy. But can we please start looking for big cat prints now?"

Over the next three evenings they gradually sat closer and closer to the bucket and when Cloud arrived Poppy kept up her chatter so he got used to the sound of her voice.

He was still hobbling but his stomach looked slightly rounder and his coat a shade less dull. He looked at them inquisitively as Poppy talked and she felt as though she was making real progress. She texted Scarlett every morning to update her, and wished the last precious days of summer away in her impatience to see Cloud each evening. She felt as though she was walking around in her own little bubble of happiness.

But on the fourth night Poppy's bubble was broken. She and Charlie arrived in the clearing and she placed the bucket on the beach, confident that Cloud would turn up as usual. But half an hour passed, then an hour, with no sign of the pony.

"Where is he?" she wailed, looking around desperately. "I thought he was beginning to trust me. Is it something I've done wrong?" Perhaps he'd been hit by a car, caught by George Blackstone or fallen down a ditch and broken his leg…

She couldn't bear the thought of leaving in case Cloud was in danger. But it was getting late and she knew Caroline would be worried. She finally admitted defeat and they trudged back home.

"I'm sure he's OK," said Charlie. "He probably went off exploring and didn't realise what time it was. It happens to me all the time."

But Poppy was on edge all evening and after a fitful night's sleep woke early. She let herself out of the house and ran all the way to the clearing. She could barely believe it when she found the bucket was empty. It gave her a glimmer of hope and made her more determined than ever to try again that night.

Charlie spent the day sneezing.

"No badger-watching for you tonight I'm afraid, angel. You need an early night," said Caroline, as they sat down at the kitchen table to eat plates of pasta. Usually Caroline made her own pasta sauce but tonight it was out of a jar.

"Can I still go? I'm sure it's only a matter of time before we see a badger," said Poppy, her face turned expectantly towards her stepmother.

She could see Caroline wavering and pressed home her advantage. "It's not far into the wood from the Riverdale fence. And I'll take my mobile with me."

"OK, but only for half an hour. It looks like rain and I don't want you going down with a cold as well, not with school starting so soon," she said.

Rolling grey clouds were chasing each other across the horizon like a herd of monstrous sheep as Poppy left the house. Once in the clearing she sat with her back against an oak tree, just a few feet from the bucket. For an agonising half an hour, worry gnawed at her insides. Then she heard a familiar rustle in the undergrowth. She was sure it was the sound of a large animal making its way closer. The rustling stopped. Poppy held her breath and waited. Branches crackled and Cloud appeared. He saw Poppy and walked straight over to the bucket. Exhaling slowly, Poppy began talking to him as he munched away quietly.

"I'm going to stand up ever so slowly and see if you'll let me stroke you. I'll be quiet and gentle and I promise I won't hurt you. I want to help you, Cloud, but you have to trust me." He looked at her, his flanks rising and falling with each breath and his ears flicking backwards and forwards. Something about the girl's voice stirred a deeply buried memory. This girl brought him food in a bucket that smelt of his old companion, the donkey who'd always made him feel safe. Cloud's leg ached and he felt tired. He could smell the first faint traces of winter in the air and he didn't feel ready for the long, cold, dark months ahead. He stood still as Poppy approached infinitesimally slowly, her eyes cast down, her voice calm and gentle. He flinched as she raised her hand to his flank but remained still as she stroked him softly, still talking to him. The outside world disappeared, leaving just the brown-haired girl and the dappled grey pony set in sharp relief against the emerald green backdrop of the trees.

"That's it, there's a good boy. You are so brave," murmured Poppy as she stroked Cloud's neck and ran her hand over his withers and ribs. She felt him relax imperceptibly under her hand and he lowered his head and looked at her. A jolt of pure euphoria shot through her body and she struggled to keep her voice steady. She remembered the packet of Polos she had brought with her but as she slowly reached into her pocket for them the silence was pierced by the harsh ringtone of her mobile phone. Cloud's head shot up, he turned on the spot and cantered unevenly off into the woods. Poppy's elation shrivelled to dust and she looked in frustration at the screen.

Riverdale calling. Caroline! Furious and resentful, she pressed the green key. "I was finally getting somewhere and you've just frightened the living daylights out of him," she hissed without thinking.

"Sweetheart, I'm just checking you're OK. It's getting late."

The hurt in Caroline's voice irritated Poppy intensely. "There was no need to phone. I'm perfectly fine," she snapped.

"Don't be like that, Poppy. I was worried about you. Are you on your way back yet? And who did I frighten the living daylights out of, anyway?"

Poppy reminded herself why she was supposed to be in the wood. "The badger, of course. I saw him close up for the first time," she lied.

"Charlie will be fed up he missed it but I'm glad you've had an exciting evening. Anyway, come home now. I don't want you out there on your own too late."

Poppy felt like stamping her feet or hollering to the skies but knew it wouldn't make any difference. As usual Caroline had borne the brunt of her anger. She picked up the bucket and took one last look at the curtain of trees through which Cloud had disappeared. A slight movement caught her eye and she squinted in the half-light, struggling to see what it was. Two soft brown eyes on a ghostly grey face were staring back at her through the branches. Her heart sang as she realised that Cloud was still there.

"You brave, brave boy. I am so proud of you. And I'll see you tomorrow, Cloud," she told him.

By the time Poppy opened the back door she was whistling cheerfully, her earlier frustration forgotten. Feeling benevolent towards Caroline she called, "I'm back! Would you like a cup of tea?"

Her stepmother walked into the kitchen and leant against the doorframe as she watched Poppy. "That would be lovely thanks, sweetheart. I was just going to make one myself."

"How's Charlie feeling? Did he -. Hold on, have you been *crying*?" asked Poppy, noticing Caroline's red-rimmed eyes.

"No, not really. Well, yes. A little," Caroline admitted. She looked discomfited and Poppy was lost for words. In all the years she had known Caroline she'd never seen her stepmother shed a single tear.

"What's wrong? It wasn't because I was cross when you rang, was it?" Poppy was incredulous.

"No. Well, not really. I've just been feeling a bit down recently and little things seem to set me off. It wasn't your fault. It's me." Caroline shrugged her shoulders and avoided Poppy's eye as she crossed the kitchen to lift two dirty mugs off the draining board before rinsing them half-heartedly under the cold tap. Poppy looked around. Her head had been so full of Cloud that she hadn't noticed until now that the kitchen was a state. Their dinner plates were still on the table and the remains of the pasta sauce had congealed like a sticky red scab around the edge of the saucepan. Caroline followed her gaze and shrugged again. "I know. It's a bit of a mess, but I was just coming out to tackle it."

Poppy said firmly, "No, you go and sit down. I'll sort this lot out and I'll bring your tea through in a minute."

To her horror Caroline looked as if she might be about to burst into tears again, so Poppy turned and started clearing the table, feeling helpless in the face of her stepmother's distress. Poppy knew Caroline well enough to know something must be very wrong and she had no idea how to fix it. As she loaded the dishwasher she wished her dad was home. He always knew what to do.

CHAPTER 16

The bright autumnal days had been replaced by a relentless September mizzle that settled on the moors like a heavy overcoat and matched Caroline's bleak mood. Poppy was feeling under pressure. There were four days left before term started and the thought of school made her sick with nerves. To make matters worse the annual drift was just over three weeks away and although she knew she was gaining Cloud's trust it was a slow process and she was no nearer to catching him.

A sneezing and coughing Charlie was banned from joining Poppy on her nightly 'badger watch' until he was over his cold. One afternoon as he sat on the end of her bed, a string of green mucus hanging from each nostril, he asked her why she didn't tell Caroline about Cloud.

"She likes horses. She used to ride when she was your age, remember?"

Poppy wasn't sure why she kept Cloud a secret, if she was honest. Caroline probably would have understood and tried to help, although the way she was at the moment she didn't really seem to care much about anything. On the plus side her stepmother's malaise meant that Poppy was enjoying much more freedom than usual. On the down side the house was a tip, the washing basket was overflowing and they were existing on frozen ready meals and jars. In Twickenham Caroline had fed the children nothing but healthy, organic food and they'd snacked on pumpkin seeds and fruit. These days she just slapped whatever happened to be in the cupboard or freezer into the oven. This week they'd had turkey twizzlers, oven chips and baked beans for three nights running. Charlie was in heaven, but Poppy was missing the ready supplies of hummous and fresh vegetables. She had a spot on her forehead and a couple of nights ago had even Googled the symptoms of scurvy.

"I will tell her. Just not yet," promised Poppy.

The next morning Charlie was feeling better and was itching to get out after being cooped up inside for so long. The rain had stopped and Poppy suggested they take a picnic lunch onto the moor. She wanted to see if they could find Cloud and Charlie was desperate to discover a paw print. Caroline, pleading the onset of a migraine, was curled up in bed with the curtains drawn when Poppy crept in. It was so out of character that Poppy was beginning to wonder if her stepmother had lost the plot.

"Caroline, would it be alright if we took a picnic up onto the tor? I promise not to let Charlie do anything silly." Poppy spoke slowly and with emphasis, as if she were talking to a half-wit. Grateful to be left in peace Caroline said they could go as long as they stayed within sight of Riverdale and had Poppy's phone with them.

There wasn't much in the cupboards but Poppy cobbled together a picnic of sausage rolls, crisps, half a packet of bourbon biscuits and the last of the raisins, in the hope that they would provide at least a small dose of vitamin C. She packed the food into her rucksack along with a couple of bottles of water, Charlie scooped up his binoculars and camera and they set off.

"The ground is nice and soft so we should be able to see any prints quite easily," said Charlie, as he hitched the camera strap up his shoulder.

"Can you also keep an eye out for Cloud's hoofprints? I'm sure he can't stay hidden in the wood all day. He must come out and graze sometimes. I was wondering if he ran with a particular herd of Dartmoor ponies," Poppy said.

They skirted around the edge of the wood at the base of the tor, inspecting the ground as they walked as if they were forensic officers examining a crime scene. Charlie found a smudged hoofprint in the mud that could have been Cloud's but could equally have belonged to one of the larger Dartmoor ponies. They came across the same herd they had seen when they first moved to Riverdale, but there was no sign of the dappled grey pony.

"Shall we have our picnic now?" suggested Poppy, and they settled down in the shelter of a large boulder. She shared out the lunch and watched her brother with amusement as he dived on the food as if he hadn't eaten for weeks. She stretched her legs out in front of her as she leant back on the boulder. "Can I borrow your binoculars, Charlie? I'll see if I can see Cloud."

Poppy adjusted the lens until the view in front of her swam into focus and she started scanning the moor, sweeping from left to right as she looked for Cloud's familiar grey shape. But the vast expanse of green and purple moorland was deserted. Not a sheep, a rambler or a pony in sight. Even the crows had stopped wheeling overhead. The air was still and silent. Odd, thought Poppy, as she reached for a handful of raisins and munched thoughtfully.

"It feels a bit weird up here today, don't you think?" she asked her brother, who was lying on his front watching a grasshopper rubbing his spindly legs against gossamer wings.

He shrugged. "What do you mean?"

"Like the calm before the storm. It's as if something's waiting to happen. Don't worry, I'm probably just imagining things." She handed Charlie the binoculars and he trained them on the grasshopper. The insect sprang away in a series of staccato leaps, making him jump.

A mosquito buzzed angrily and Poppy waved it away. The air felt sticky and she could feel a slick of sweat across her forehead. "Come on, let's make a move," she told her brother. But Charlie was sitting as still as a statue, staring at the top of the tor. When she followed his gaze her hand flew to her mouth. Tucked behind another huge boulder was a black, distinctly feline-shaped head with small pointed ears and a jutting jaw.

"Look at that!" breathed Charlie. Poppy motioned to his camera. "Take a picture. Quickly!" she said in sotto voce. He lifted the camera, zoomed in as far as he could and pressed the shutter a dozen times. The animal looked in their direction then jumped with a neat spring onto the rock.

"Oh no, the battery's run out," said Charlie. He swapped the camera for his binoculars and they watched as, with a flick of its long tail, the panther-like creature bounded off the rock with one graceful leap and disappeared behind the tor. Brother and sister looked at each other in disbelief.

Charlie was the first to speak. "Poppy, this is just amazing. A big cat, living on our tor! Tell me I'm not dreaming. You did see it too, didn't you?" he asked her, suddenly uncertain.

"I saw something, goodness only knows what, but it did look like a cat," she admitted. "We need to go home and look at those photos." She shoved the remains of their picnic into her rucksack and they scrambled down the rock-strewn hill towards Riverdale.

Caroline was in the kitchen tidying up unenthusiastically.

"Mum! You're not going to believe this! We've found a big cat," shouted Charlie.

"Really? Well, that is exciting. Was it a lion, a tiger or a leopard?"

"No, we really did see one, didn't we Poppy?" He glanced at his sister for reassurance and Poppy looked at Caroline. "We saw something large and black. I don't know what it was but it definitely wasn't a sheep or a Dartmoor pony. But Charlie's taken some pictures so we can show you."

Caroline was glad of a distraction after spending the morning trying and failing to shift the feelings of lethargy and unhappiness that at times threatened to drown her. She took out her laptop, booted it up and slipped in the memory card from Charlie's camera. Together they watched the screen as Caroline downloaded the photos. There was the tor, so familiar to them by now. Charlie pointed to the boulder where they had seen the animal. "Look! There it is," he cried with relief.

Indistinct though it was, they could definitely make out the cat-shaped head. Poppy gasped. "There - look. You can see its tail." And sure enough, a long black tail stuck out from the side of the rock.

"Well I never," said Caroline in amazement. "That really is extraordinary. I wonder if it could be a panther or something?"

"Of course it is!" replied Charlie hotly. "I told you there were big cats on Dartmoor and I was right. This must be the same one Scarlett's dad saw. He'd believe me," he said, his bottom lip wobbling.

"I believe you, Charlie," said Poppy quietly. Although they had been a couple of hundred metres away she was in no doubt that what they'd seen was some kind of large cat.

"What do we do now?" demanded her brother, who was jumping from one foot to another, his blond hair tousled and his blue eyes shining.

"What do you mean?" Caroline asked, puzzled.

"Well, do we call the police or the zoo - or do we start building the big cat trap I designed ages ago?"

"I suppose we could call the Tavistock Herald," Caroline suggested. She had started out as a junior reporter on a local paper before moving to the BBC and knew they loved a big cat story - especially if there was a photo involved. The fact that a six-year-old had been behind the lens was the icing on the cake.

"Yesssss!" Charlie punched the air with his fist. "Fantastic idea, Mum. Can we do it now?"

"Sweetheart, it's gone five o'clock. There won't be anyone in the newsroom until the morning, but we'll do it then, I promise."

The intrigue brightened Caroline's mood and they

spent a happy evening playing Monopoly and eating crisps in front of the fire. It was almost like old times and Poppy felt some of the unease she had been feeling about her stepmother's frame of mind lifting.

"I really must do a big food shop tomorrow. We'll pop into the Herald offices afterwards if you like," Caroline offered and Charlie beamed.

"Is there any chance I could go and see Tory while you two are at the supermarket? I wanted to apologise for not saying goodbye when she came for tea. With school starting on Monday I'm not going to get another chance for ages," Poppy said.

"Yes, that's fine. But I still don't understand what happened between the two of you. I can't imagine Tory upsetting anyone; she's so lovely."

Poppy swallowed. Admitting she was wrong was not something she was good at. "It was my fault. She was trying to help and I was mean to her. But I don't want to talk about it," and, avoiding an inquiring look from Caroline, she picked up the dice, threw them and landed herself in jail.

CHAPTER 17

This time Poppy was prepared when she turned up at the old people's flats and walked straight bang into Mrs Parker.

"You're back, I see," said the warden, who was wearing a fitted Royal blue suit with hefty shoulder pads that matched her newly blue-rinsed hair.

"Yes, I certainly am," said Poppy firmly. She'd decided that morning to take no nonsense from the old battleaxe. "So is Tory in?"

Mrs Parker was taken aback by the girl's assertiveness. "Well, I dare say she is as her ladyship hasn't stepped foot outside her flat for the last week. She even missed her card night on Friday. Not that it was any loss. I convinced everyone to try a few hands of bridge instead of that dreadful poker she insists on playing. So much more *appropriate*," she sniffed.

"She's not ill is she?" asked Poppy, lines of concern furrowing her forehead.

"No, she's not ill, but she's not herself," conceded Mrs Parker. "Not that she'll tell me what's wrong, of course. Says I shouldn't stick my nose in, I ask you. Perhaps you'll have more luck."

Poppy headed down the corridor towards Tory's front door. She knocked and waited. She heard the volume of the television being turned down and the sound of shuffling. She rehearsed her apology one last time.

Tory opened the door. "Ah, Poppy. Come in." Poppy felt that the welcome was more muted than before and she cursed herself for her behaviour. After all, her friend had only been trying to help. She started gabbling an apology but Tory held up a hand to silence her.

"It's alright, pet. Everyone says things they don't mean every now and then. The fact that you've come to say sorry is enough for me. Let's forget it ever happened."

Flushed with gratitude, Poppy realised that she could learn a lot from Tory. She sat down and they chatted about the weather and school and Poppy told Tory about the cat-like animal they had seen the previous day.

Tory wasn't surprised. "I've never seen any big cats myself, but it's true that people used to have leopards and panthers in private collections. Then local councils decided they needed licences to keep them and I dare say a few were released into the wild. I bet Charlie's pleased."

"You're not wrong there. He's beyond excited. He hasn't stopped talking about it, and now he's convinced he's going to be front page news in the Herald. He'll be unbearable," said Poppy, not minding in the least.

She thought of Caroline staring mindlessly out of the kitchen window and remembered why she had come. "Tory, I need to talk to you about something."

"Is it Cloud?"

"No. Actually I want to ask your advice about Caroline."

Tory raised her eyebrows. This was a turn up for the books. "What's the matter, pet?"

"You were right and I'm sorry again for storming off. I've noticed Caroline hasn't been herself and since the day you came to lunch she's been even worse. The house is a tip, she's feeding us non-stop junk food and I keep finding her just staring out of the window. She always used to be so cheerful. Annoyingly cheerful, most of the time. But it's like we've got her identical twin living with us. She looks the same, she sounds the same, but this one doesn't seem to care about anything. And she's forgotten how to smile."

Poppy breathed out deeply, relieved to have voiced the concerns that had been building over the past few weeks.

"I think she's probably suffering from depression,"

said Tory matter-of-factly. "Has she ever been like this before?"

"Never. But I had a friend at school whose mum was depressed and had to take tablets for it. She called them her happy pills."

"They're called antidepressants. I had post natal depression after Jo was born, although we didn't call it that in those days, it was just the baby blues." Poppy looked at Tory in surprise. "It's more common than you think, you know. But it is treatable. We'll keep an eye on her for a couple of weeks and if she's still no better perhaps we need to convince her to go to see her GP."

Poppy smiled at Tory gratefully. "Thank you. I didn't want to worry Dad – he's too far away to do anything anyway. And Charlie's too young to notice anything's wrong. He's just happy to have chips for tea every night."

"I'm glad to help, pet. And if you are in the slightest bit worried about Caroline phone me. Don't feel as though you have to sort it all out on your own. I'll do whatever I can to help. Now, should you be making a move? I don't want to make you late for Caroline and Charlie."

Poppy said goodbye, glad that she and Tory were friends again, and set off for the café where she had arranged to meet her stepmother and brother.

"They're going to send a reporter and a photographer to interview us tomorrow!" Charlie said, the moment she sat down.

"Us?" she replied, puzzled. This was Charlie's obsession, not hers.

"You were there, too. I'm only six so they want you there to collaborate my story," he said importantly.

"Corroborate," corrected Caroline gently and Poppy stole a quick look at her stepmother. There were still dark shadows under her eyes and she looked wan, but at least she seemed to be interested in the big cat story. Perhaps she was over the worst.

Later that afternoon Poppy cornered Charlie in his bedroom, where he was making a complicated three dimensional version of his big cat trap with Lego and K'Nex.

"You need to help me clean the house before the people from the Herald come tomorrow. It's a pigsty," she told him.

Normally the mere suggestion of helping around the house invoked a storm of protest, but Charlie was so excited about the reporter's arrival that, for once, he was happy to oblige.

"I'll do the kitchen. You can make a start on the lounge. We'll get up early tomorrow and do it. It'll be a nice surprise for Caroline," said Poppy. Unaccountably the thought of helping her stepmother gave her a warm, fuzzy feeling. It was too weird for words.

CHAPTER 18

Charlie was as good as his word and the next morning he was already sitting at the kitchen table eating a bowl of cereal when Poppy came in from feeding Chester. She gave him the beeswax polish, a duster and a set of instructions.

"The first job is to tidy up. The old newspapers can go in the recycling bin and put any grubby clothes you find in the washing basket. I'll put a wash on later." Poppy eyed a dirty sock, lolling like a diseased rodent under the sofa. "Bring the dirty mugs, glasses and plates into the kitchen and plump up the cushions on the sofa and chairs. Then you can dust. Once you've done that I'll bring you the vacuum cleaner. By the time you've finished the place should look like new. Got all that?"

"Yes," said Charlie, counting the jobs off on his

fingers. "I'm to put the grubby clothes in the recycling, polish the glasses and plump up the newspapers. Only joking," he added hastily, seeing the exasperated expression on his sister's face.

It took almost an hour for Poppy to load the dishwasher, wipe down the surfaces, clean the sink, empty the bin and sweep and clean the kitchen floor. She was pleasantly surprised when she went into the lounge to inspect Charlie's handiwork. The wooden floor gleamed and the rug in front of the fire was no longer covered with crumbs. Cushions had been plumped and the mess tidied away. Charlie was beaming with pride.

"Well done, little bro. Caroline will be pleased."

"I certainly am." Caroline's voice made Poppy jump. She was standing at the doorway, with a smile on her face that for once reached her eyes. "The kitchen and lounge look amazing. Aren't you two good to me. Come here, let me give you both a hug."

Charlie ran straight into her arms. Poppy hesitated. Being the outsider was her default setting, the part she had chosen to play. But Caroline beckoned her close and she found herself walking slowly over, as if pulled by an invisible thread.

"Thank-you, darling, I expect it was all your doing. What a lovely surprise," she murmured into Poppy's hair as she held the two children close.

"It was Poppy's idea. I just did what I was told, as usual," admitted Charlie with a grin. "I did a good job though, didn't I? Did you see how shiny the floor is now?"

For once Poppy allowed herself to relax into her stepmother's embrace. The three of them clung together until Charlie started fidgeting and wriggled out of their arms. Caroline took Poppy's face in her hands and tilted it up to hers. "You don't know how much that means to me. Thank-you, sweetheart," she said softly, and kissed her forehead before letting her go. Poppy wasn't sure if Caroline was referring to the clean-up operation or the hug, but realised that for once it didn't actually matter.

A rap at the door sent Charlie into orbit. "They're here! They're here! Quick, where's the photo?" he shouted, and they swung into action, Caroline going to answer the door, Poppy grabbing the laptop from the dining room and Charlie bouncing off the walls in excitement.

The reporter and photographer from the Tavistock Herald were waiting on the doorstep with polite smiles on their faces.

"Mrs McKeever?" inquired the shorter of the two. He glanced down at his notebook. "And you must be Charlie and Poppy. I'm Stanley Smith, though people call me Sniffer. And this is our photographer Henry Blossom, though people call him Henry." No-one smiled at the joke.

"Pleased to meet you," said the photographer, who was a tall, thin man with a camera slung around his neck, a camera bag on his shoulder and a long-suffering expression on his face. Caroline shook their hands and they followed her into the lounge, Charlie and Poppy in their wake.

"So, we'll have a chat and then go out onto the moor to see where you said you saw this 'ere puma, shall we?" said Sniffer, winking at Charlie.

"I didn't say I saw the cat, I actually saw it. And I don't think it was a puma, I think it was a jaguar," answered Charlie with spirit, and Poppy saw shades of their dad in her brother. Charlie may have only been six, but he wasn't about to be patronised by a middle-aged hack from a local paper, not when his dad was a famous war correspondent for the BBC. Sniffer didn't endear himself to either of the children when he shoved a sleeping Magpie off the comfiest of the armchairs so he could sit down. The cat shot him a look of pure disdain and stalked off to the corner of the room, where he proceeded to wash himself, stopping every now and then to look daggers at the reporter.

"Tell me what happened on Thursday then, Charlie," Sniffer said, thumbing through his notebook until he reached a blank page.

Charlie recounted how they'd decided to have a picnic on their tor. "Usually there are sheep everywhere but on Thursday there weren't any. I thought that was a bit strange."

Poppy couldn't remember Charlie saying as much at the time, but she kept the thought to herself. She didn't want to rain on his parade.

"Anyway, we were just about to go when

something caught my eye. I saw the head of a big cat poking up from behind this huge boulder. I told Poppy to look and I got out my camera and took some photos. Then the cat jumped onto the boulder and we got a really good look at it. It was massive!" said Charlie.

"Unfortunately the camera battery ran out before the animal jumped onto the rock, but Charlie did manage to take a few pictures before it packed up," said Caroline, swivelling the laptop so the two men could see the screen. They both leant forward, poring over the photos. Within seconds the scepticism vanished from Sniffer's face.

"Interesting, very interesting," he said, half to himself. He turned to Charlie. "You could have something here, young man. I have contacts on the nationals and they love a genuine big cat story. We might get some mileage from this."

"Don't forget where your loyalties lie, Stanley," said Henry. "The Herald has the exclusive."

Fortunately Caroline knew the ways of local journalists who liked to make a bit of extra cash selling stories to the national newspapers. "And you'll not be forgetting that these are Charlie's pictures, taken on Charlie's camera and are therefore his copyright," she said pleasantly.

A nasty expression flitted across Sniffer's face, although Henry Blossom looked at her admiringly. "Too true, Mrs McKeever," he said, in his gentle Devon burr. "I'll make sure no-one takes advantage of him," he added, eyeing his colleague pointedly. Caroline smiled her thanks and the five of them headed outside and up onto the tor, where Henry took pictures of Charlie and Poppy by the boulder where they'd seen the big cat.

"When will the story be in the paper?" demanded Charlie.

"I want to show the photos to the head cat keeper at the local zoo first to get his take on them. But the story should make the next edition," replied Sniffer.

"Cool! Do you think I'll end up on the telly like my dad?"

Sniffer stood stock still, his eyes fixed on Charlie. He reminded Poppy of a hound that had just picked up the scent of a fox. "Who's your dad then, young man?" the reporter asked, thinking privately that this story was getting better and better.

"Mike McKeever. He's a war correspondent for the BBC," Charlie said proudly.

Sniffer took a pen from behind his ear and made a few more indecipherable squiggles in his notebook. "Good, good. Right then, Henry. We'd better be heading back."

"Are you sure you wouldn't like a cup of tea first?" asked Caroline.

"Aye, that would be champion, Mrs McKeever," said Henry Blossom, slinging his camera bag over his shoulder and giving Caroline a wide smile. Poppy noticed that he had a lop-sided gait, the result of years spent hefting about bags laden with lenses.

Back at the house Caroline switched on the kettle and disappeared into the lounge to light the fire. Henry and Charlie joined Poppy in the kitchen. Sniffer stood outside the back door among a pile of abandoned wellies trying, without much success, to get a signal on his mobile phone. Poppy was setting out a row of mugs and dropping a teabag in each when she heard a cry and an almighty crash from the lounge. Her stomach flipped over. Henry and Charlie stopped talking and were rooted to the spot. Poppy dropped the teabags and rushed into the lounge. Caroline was lying on the wooden floor, clutching her left wrist. Her face was white. "I think I've broken my arm. It's the floor – it's so slippery," she gasped.

Poppy took a look and flinched. Caroline's hand was bent at an unnatural angle to her arm and her wrist was already starting to swell. She looked as if she was about to pass out. Suddenly the reassuring presence of Henry Blossom loomed behind them. "Oh dear. What have we here?" he said in his gentle voice.

Assessing the situation in a flash, he started giving instructions. "Right Poppy, where's the phone? I think we're probably going to need an ambulance. Charlie, you go and find a blanket for your mum. We don't want her going into shock."

He knelt down beside Caroline. "I think it's safe to say you've broken your wrist. And a proper job you've made of it too, by the looks of things. We're going to call an ambulance. You're going to need to go to hospital. And the paramedics will be able to give you something for the pain."

"What about the children?" whispered Caroline, as Henry took a patchwork blanket from Charlie's hands and wrapped it gently around her shoulders.

"Don't you worry. I'll stay with them until we get something sorted. I'll get Sniffer to ring the boss and let her know. She'll understand. Is there anyone else who can look after them until you get back from hospital?"

"My husband's in the Middle East. I could ask my sister but she has children of her own and lives in Bromley anyway. It would take her hours to get here."

Poppy thought. "What about Tory? She'd come and look after us."

"Tory Wickens? Do you have her number, Poppy? I'll give her a ring once the ambulance is here and arrange for her to come over," said Henry.

Satisfied with the arrangements Caroline slumped down against the sofa and they waited together in silence for the ambulance.

CHAPTER 19

The next few hours passed by in a blur. The ambulance arrived and two cheery paramedics took charge, strapping Caroline's wrist into a sling and giving her gas and air for the pain. Henry Blossom was as good as his word and phoned Tory, who promised to ring her nephew at once to bring her over. Sniffer prowled around the lounge, picking up photos of the McKeevers and examining the family's assorted curios and ornaments, from fossils found by the children to Caroline's collection of old Chinese vases. Poppy watched the journalist, seeing the room through his eyes. Caroline had spent a week painting the walls and sanding and waxing the floorboards. Two huge squashy damson-coloured sofas, a battered leather armchair and their eclectic collection of painted furniture were arranged around the open fireplace. Patchwork throws and cushions the colour of jewels made the room warm and welcoming. Poppy realised with a jolt that Riverdale already felt more of a home to her than their house in Twickenham ever had.

Her stepmother's face was still ashen as the paramedics accompanied her to the ambulance. Grimacing with pain at every step, Caroline thanked Henry, who had promised to stay with Poppy and Charlie until Tory arrived. Caroline turned to the children, who both looked slightly shell-shocked. "Goodbye, angels. I'll be back as soon as I can. Be good for Tory, won't you?"

"Of course we will!" said Charlie, slipping his hand into Poppy's. "Anyway, Poppy will look after me, won't you Poppy?" He looked at his big sister trustingly.

Poppy smiled into his blue eyes, so like Caroline's, and her heart gave a funny twist. She squeezed his hand and replied, "It goes without saying, little brother." She looked shyly at Caroline. "I hope everything goes OK at the hospital. Will you ring and let us know how you get on?"

"Of course I will, sweetheart. Don't you worry about me – I'll be fine." And she stepped gingerly into the ambulance and was gone.

"Your mum's a brave lass," observed Henry. For the first time in her life Poppy didn't feel the urge to correct him. "Yes, she is," she said quietly.

While they waited for Tory to arrive Poppy finished

making Henry's cup of tea and went into the lounge to straighten the rug where Caroline had fallen. As she walked over to the window she, too, almost lost her footing. The floor was as slippery as an ice rink. She looked at the gleaming wooden floorboards and suddenly everything was clear. Poppy tracked her brother down in his bedroom, where he was morosely lining up his action heroes in height order.

"Charlie – when you tidied the lounge this morning, how did you clean the floor?" she asked gently.

"I hoovered the rug and used that polish you gave me on the wooden bit of the floor of course," he said, not looking up from his toys.

"I thought so," said Poppy. "Probably best not to use polish on the floor again next time. Makes it a bit slippy," she added, as tactfully as she could. "I think I'd better go and wash it off before Tory arrives. We don't want her taking a tumble as well."

Charlie was humming tunelessly to himself, his head bent over the Incredible Hulk and his red Power Ranger. Poppy left him to it. There was no point making him feel guilty for causing Caroline's fall – he'd only been trying to help. Caroline would see the funny side, she felt sure.

Poppy's stomach was beginning a low level rumbling by the time she heard the crunch of gravel and a knock at the front door. She flew into the hall and threw the door open. There on the doorstep was Tory, leaning on her sticks, a look of concern on her weathered old face. Behind her, her nephew was unloading carrier bags from the boot of his car.

"Hello Poppy, I thought you might not have much in the house so we popped into the supermarket on our way. That's why we're a bit late."

"Fantastic! I'm starving. In fact I'm so hungry I could eat a Dartmoor pony!" said Charlie, who had appeared in the hallway. "Only joking – it would probably be a bit chewy. What have you got us for tea?"

Henry had followed Charlie into the hall. Poppy noticed that he walked with a stoop even when he wasn't carrying his camera bag.

"Hello Tory, long time no see," he said, holding out his hand.

"Come here, you daft twit. Give me a hug," Tory commanded, and Henry, looking slightly abashed, did as he was told. Tory watched the children's astonished faces with amusement. "I've known Henry since he was a baby," she said. "His mother was a great friend of mine. I met Margaret in the maternity ward and Jo and Henry were born within hours of each other. We always hoped they'd end up getting married but it wasn't to be," she said wistfully.

They chatted for a while until Tory's nephew started making noises about getting back before it got too dark and Henry reluctantly stood up and said he should also make a move.

"Now are you sure you're going to be OK looking after the children, Tory? Will you be able to manage the stairs?" he asked.

"I lived here on my own until the beginning of July, Henry Blossom," she replied tartly. "We'll be absolutely fine. Poppy can show me where everything is, can't you, pet?"

They waved the two cars off and went into the kitchen where Tory, with Poppy acting as her sous chef, cooked sausages and mash with peas and onion gravy.

"That was yum," declared Charlie, yawning extravagantly. He stuck his thumb in his mouth and watched sleepily while Tory cleared the table and Poppy began loading the dishwasher. Poppy felt a wave of responsibility sweep over her. Both children were so used to their dad's trips abroad that his absences were part of the fabric of family life, but Caroline was a permanent fixture. The only time Poppy could recall her stepmother being away for any length of time was when she went into hospital to have Charlie six-and-a-half years ago.

Poppy remembered how excited everyone had been, how they assumed she was looking forward to the baby coming. Truth was, she'd dreaded it. The thought of another girl coming into their home and commanding all her dad's attention was beyond endurance. When she found out the interloper was a boy it was a little easier to bear and, despite initial resistance on her part, her baby brother gradually wormed his way into her affections. Charlie was an easy baby with a gummy smile that sent old ladies into clucky raptures. But he only had eyes for one person – his big sister. His blue eyes followed Poppy adoringly around the room and as soon as he could crawl he became her shadow. Occasionally having a kid brother got on her nerves but after five years as an only child it was nice to always have someone to play with, even if the games did tend to involve trains and super heroes.

"Come on Charlie. Let's take you to bed before you fall asleep at the table," she said now, and he followed her obediently up to his room.

By the time she came back down half an hour later Tory was settled on one of the sofas with some knitting, the clicking needles the only sound. Poppy looked at the clock on the oak beam above the fireplace. It was almost eight o'clock and too late to go and see Cloud now. The day had been so filled with drama that she hadn't given the pony a second thought for hours, she realised guiltily.

"We never did get a chance to talk about Cloud, did we? Have you seen him again?" Tory said, as if reading her mind.

Poppy played with a strand of her hair while she deliberated whether or not to tell Tory about her attempts to catch the pony and hide him from the drift. Deciding they both had Cloud's best interests at heart she took the plunge and told Tory about her forays into the wood under the pretext of badger-watching, the pony's poor condition and the buckets of food he had wolfed down.

"The last few times I've really felt I've made progress. He's let me stroke him and I'm sure he's beginning to trust me. But the drift is only two weeks away and I start school on Monday. I'm running out of time," she said despondently. Tory stopped knitting and her eyes took on a faraway look. Poppy thought back to the conversation Caroline had overheard in the post office all those weeks ago. Tory must have hidden the pony every autumn to stop him being rounded up with the rest of the Dartmoor ponies.

"Tory?" she began, biting her bottom lip until it turned white.

"Yes, pet?" The needles resumed their rhythmic clicking.

"I know you'd have hated it if Cloud had ended up back at George Blackstone's farm. I was wondering…did you hide him here at Riverdale?"

Tory stopped knitting again and looked at Poppy. She reminded her so much of Caitlyn and it was clear to her that Poppy and Cloud had some kind of connection, just as Caitlyn and Cloud had once had. Taking a deep breath, Tory made a decision she hoped she wouldn't live to regret.

"Yes, pet, I did. Saving her beloved Cloud was the one thing I could still do for Caitlyn, so that's what I did."

"But he's so nervous around people. How on earth did you manage to catch him?"

Tory smiled sadly. "Think about it logically, Poppy.

The answer is right under your nose."

CHAPTER 20

"What do you mean?" asked Poppy.

Tory laid her knitting on her lap. "I think I told you that when Cloud first arrived at Riverdale he was incredibly nervous around people?"

Poppy nodded.

"Gaining his trust took a long time. He spent the first few days cowering in the corner of his stable. Caitlyn spent hours sitting in there with him, trying to tempt him closer with carrots and Polos, but he wouldn't go near her. I was beginning to think I'd made a terrible mistake, although Caitlyn refused to give up on him. But then someone you know very well helped us make the breakthrough." Her eyes twinkled.

"Chester?" breathed Poppy.

"Yes," smiled Tory. "Of course he was much

younger in those days and loved to be at the centre of things. While Caitlyn sat in the corner of Cloud's stable Chester would rest his head over the stable door, watching this dappled grey bag of nerves in the corner. Chester had an amazingly calming effect on Cloud and as time went on Cloud gradually came out of his shell and started to trust us all. By the time Caitlyn was able to handle Cloud he and Chester were inseparable. Chester was by Cloud's side when we first tacked him up, when we long-reined him, lunged him and when Cait eventually rode him for the first time." Tory could still picture the pony and donkey standing side by side at the paddock gate as they waited patiently for Caitlyn to arrive at Riverdale.

"It meant that when Cait and Cloud started competing we always had to take Chester too, but Chester didn't mind – he thought it was a great adventure. He became a familiar sight at all the local shows and loved the attention. And as long as Cloud had Chester and Caitlyn he was alright."

"So how did Chester help you catch Cloud?"

"That first autumn after Caitlyn died I knew I had to hide Cloud from the drift so he didn't end up back at Blackstone's. So I went out onto the moor to try to catch him."

Poppy held her breath.

"I'd seen him in the distance once or twice so I thought he had stayed fairly close to Riverdale, whether to be near Chester or in the hope that Caitlyn would come back for him one day I'll never know."

Tory sniffed loudly. "But try as I might, he wouldn't let me near him. Then one night not long before the drift I was lying awake in bed worrying what to do when I heard Chester braying and suddenly I had the answer."

"So you took Chester out onto the moor to see if Cloud would follow him home?"

"That's exactly what I did. The very next morning Chester and I went to the end of Riverdale wood. You know where the trees start to peter out at the foot of the tor?"

Poppy nodded. It was close to where she and Charlie had seen the big cat.

"Apart from a few sheep it was deserted but I had a funny feeling that Cloud would turn up. We waited for over an hour before he finally appeared. I think he'd been hiding in the trees watching us for a while. He and Chester were so pleased to see each other and when I started leading Chester home Cloud followed, all the way back into Chester's stable where he stayed until after the drift. That's how I caught him."

"But why did you let him go again once the drift was over?" demanded Poppy.

"It was the right thing to do. He belonged to George Blackstone, don't forget. Keeping him would have been theft. But every year Chester and I led him back to Riverdale and kept him safe."

"What did you think would happen to him this year, Tory?"

The old woman sighed. "It's been worrying me for

months, pet. What with leaving Riverdale, missing Chester so much and fretting about Cloud I haven't really been myself." She looked close to tears.

"Couldn't someone have helped you?" Poppy asked more gently.

"I thought about trying to talk to Jo, to see if she would, but she hasn't spoken to me for years and she still blames Cloud for Cait's death anyway. She wouldn't throw a bucket of water on him if he was on fire. I can't stop thinking how disappointed Caitlyn would have been in me."

Poppy wasn't a demonstrative child but Tory looked so desolate that she reached over and hugged her. Tory batted away a couple of tears that were rolling slowly down her lined face and muttered, 'Don't mind me, pet'. She smelt of talcum powder and peppermint and her jumper, the colour of heather, felt as soft as down against Poppy's cheek. She only drew back when she realised that one of Tory's knitting needles was poking uncomfortably in her ribcage.

"You have me now. I'll take Chester out onto the moor to see Cloud and we'll bring him back to Riverdale together."

Tory was about to reply when the phone rang. "It'll probably be Caroline," said Poppy, dashing over to the oak sideboard and grabbing the handset.

"Poppy, it's me," said her stepmother. She sounded echoey - as if she was standing in the middle of a vast aircraft hangar. "They've brought a phone to my bed.

I'm in the orthopaedic ward. It's full of young men who've fallen off their motorbikes. But they're all very chatty," she added inconsequentially. Poppy wondered how many painkillers Caroline had been given.

"So how's your wrist?" she asked.

"Oh, that. They've X-rayed it and it's a clean break, luckily. They finished plastering it about half an hour ago. I am now officially plastered," she laughed. Poppy raised her eyebrows. "But unfortunately I must have banged my head when I fell because they say I've got mild concussion. Anyway, enough of me. How are you and Charlie?"

"Oh, Charlie's happy – he's gone to bed on a full stomach. I'm keeping Tory company," she smiled at her old friend, who had taken up her needles again and was poised to start clicking. "Do you know when you'll be back?" Poppy asked, thinking of her plans for the morning.

"They're going to keep me in for the night because of the concussion. Will you all be OK? I'm going to try and ring your dad now to see if there's any chance he can come home early. In fact I'd better try now before I run out of credit. I'll ring you again in the morning to let you know when I'll be back. Night night darling." And the phone went dead.

"Everything alright?" Tory asked.

"Yes, she seems a bit spaced out but otherwise fine. Much more cheerful, actually. It sounds as though she should be back some time tomorrow. So I've decided.

Chester and I are going to bring Cloud home tomorrow morning before she gets back."

Before she went to bed Poppy let herself out of the back door, slipped on her wellies and went to see Chester. She flicked a switch and the single bulb hanging from the roof cast a yellow glow over the stable where he stood chewing hay.

"You and I have an important job to do tomorrow," she told the donkey, rubbing his velvety soft nose. A kaleidoscope of butterflies was sending her stomach into turmoil as nerves and excitement started to build.

Chester, completely oblivious to the rescue mission ahead of them, eyed her calmly and carried on munching.

CHAPTER 21

Poppy woke late after a fitful night's sleep. When she'd finally managed to doze off she'd dreamt of black panthers stalking grey ponies to a soundtrack of rushing water. Opening the curtains she realised why – heavy rain was falling in sheets from a thundery grey sky. The tor was completely concealed by low cloud curling around the trees at the edge of the Riverdale wood. Poppy gave an involuntary shiver. It was what Caroline called Hound of the Baskervilles weather. Unable to shift a sense of unease that had inexplicably settled on her like the mist on the tor, she followed the smell of toast downstairs and into the kitchen where Tory was unloading the dishwasher.

"Hello Poppy, there you are. I thought I'd leave you to lie in. Thought you needed a decent night's sleep after the dramas of yesterday," she said.

Poppy glanced at the clock on the oven. Ten to nine. "Has Charlie had his breakfast already?" she asked, sitting down at the kitchen table.

"No, pet. I didn't want to disturb him either. Poor lamb looked all in last night. He's having a lie in, too."

"Crikey. I don't think I've ever known Charlie to stay in bed past seven o'clock. Usually he's the first up."

Poppy yawned and smiled her thanks at Tory as the old woman placed a plate of buttered toast in front of her, although the butterflies in her stomach made the thought of eating impossible.

"I don't think it's a good idea to go out on the moor today, Poppy. Dartmoor can be a dangerous place at the best of times, but in weather like this it's treacherous. I'd never forgive myself if anything happened to you or Charlie while I'm looking after you both."

Poppy was silent. There was no way a bit of rain was going to stop her rescuing Cloud, but she didn't want to worry Tory. "Perhaps it'll brighten up later," she ventured.

"Perhaps," replied Tory, unconvinced. "What would you like to do this morning? Shall I teach you poker?"

"Yes, that would be fun. Thanks for breakfast but I'm not really hungry. I'll go and clean my teeth and then feed Chester," she said.

On her way back from the bathroom Poppy glanced into Charlie's bedroom and saw the silhouette

of his sleeping shape under the Thomas the Tank
Engine duvet cover that, aged six, he now considered
too babyish for words. She went back downstairs, fed
Chester, then spent a companionable hour with Tory
learning about flushes and five card draws, poker
faces and tells. When ten o'clock had been and gone
and there was still no sign of her brother Poppy put
down yet another losing hand and said, "Tory, before
you beat me again, I'm going to check on Charlie. I
won't be a minute."

She crept into Charlie's room and peered into his
bed. Expecting to see his tousled blond head on the
pillow, his thumb in his mouth, she gasped in shock
when she saw the head of his biggest teddy bear
instead. She whipped off the duvet and found
Caroline's fluffy cream dressing gown laying rolled up
where her sleeping brother should have been. She
looked wildly about the room as if he was going to
jump out of his wardrobe and surprise her with a
triumphant 'Gotcha!' But there was no sign of the six-
year-old, just the usual jumble of dirty clothes, bits of
Lego scattered like fallen leaves and the line of action
heroes he'd set up the previous afternoon, their
moulded plastic faces inscrutable. Her eyes fell on a
piece of paper on his pillow. It must have slipped
underneath the bear's head when she pulled off the
duvet. Scrawled in Charlie's spidery handwriting was
one word. Poppy.

She grabbed the note, unfolded it and, with
mounting anxiety, read:

Deer Poppy,

I don't think sniffer bel, beleaf, believed me when I said I had seen a real live big cat. I have gone to find it and get a better picture for the paper. I have taken some sausages to use as bait. I will be back before tea.

Charlie'

Poppy grabbed a handful of the dressing gown and lifted it to her cheek. The soft towelling smelt of Caroline and she clung to it, wishing her calm, capable stepmother was downstairs and not in a hospital bed ten miles away. Magpie padded softly into the room and jumped up next to Poppy. The cat had an uncanny knack of making an appearance whenever anything interesting was happening. His two stomachs swinging beneath him, Magpie regarded Poppy with interest, waiting for her next move.

"You know what they say about curiosity, Magpie," muttered Poppy under her breath.

What should she do? The moor was no place for a daredevil six-year-old on a day like today. She didn't want to worry Tory, of that she was certain. She had no idea how long Charlie had been gone but he may not have got far. In an instant she made up her mind.

"I'll go after him," she whispered to the cat, who was now settling down for yet another nap, making himself comfortable on Caroline's dressing gown. He tucked his head beneath his tail and within seconds was snoring softly, his stomachs rising and falling in time to his breathing. Poppy ran into her room, grabbed her thickest fleece top and pulled on another pair of socks. She could hear the television in the lounge. Tory was obviously watching daytime TV. Perfect. She stole down the stairs, took her waterproof coat and wellies and quietly opened the back door.

Her heart sank when she heard the television go silent. "Poppy, is that you?" called Tory from the sofa. Poppy took a deep breath, slipped off her boots and walked into the lounge. Smiling brightly, she said, "Charlie's still comatose. I'm going to muck out Chester's stable before the weather gets any worse. Then perhaps we can have another couple of hands of poker?"

Tory looked out of the lounge window. Although mid-morning it was as dark as dusk. "Alright, pet. Don't be long though. You'll get drenched."

Practising her best poker face Poppy nodded. "OK. I'll be as quick as I can," she promised, her fingers crossed behind her back.

She grabbed a couple of lead ropes from the tack room and the torch she kept on the windowsill in case there was ever a power cut. She didn't really know why – it just made her feel a bit better prepared. Like a Girl Guide or one of the Dartmoor search and rescue people, only on a bad day.

"Wish me luck, Chester." The donkey gave her a friendly nudge and she set off into the gloom. The rain was sleeting down. Poppy pulled the hood of her jacket over her head and wished she'd worn waterproof trousers. The boulder where she and

Charlie had seen the big cat seemed as good a place as any to start her search, so she set off towards the tor, her chin tucked into her chest.

It was hard going. There was no wind but the fog and rain were all-consuming and visibility was down to three or four metres. Following her instinct she found the spot where she and Charlie had eaten their makeshift picnic just a few days before. It felt like a lifetime ago. She started calling his name, but the swirling fog deadened the noise so she stopped shouting and kept walking, stumbling over rocks and tussocks. The ground was so marshy in places that once she almost lost her boot to the peaty mire which threatened to swallow her rubber-clad foot like quicksand. She looked out for familiar landmarks but realised the fog was playing with her senses when she walked past the same twisted tree twice. Or was it a different tree? She couldn't tell any more.

Poppy felt a bubble of panic rising in her throat but she knew she had to carry on until she'd found Charlie. The two lead ropes hung like chains around her neck and her mud-covered boots felt as heavy as lead. She was saturated from head to foot. Keep walking, she told herself.

She had lost all sense of time and when she turned on the torch to look at her watch she realised with frustration that she'd left it in her bedroom. She had no idea if she'd been on the moor for one hour or three. Tory must have twigged that she had gone by now. She must also have seen Charlie's empty bed. If she'd read his note she would have put two and two together and realised that Poppy had gone in search of her brother. Would she have called the police or the search and rescue people by now? Were they at this very moment preparing to launch a search for the two children? Poppy felt terrible for putting Tory in such a difficult situation. She trudged on. By her reckoning she had walked around the base of the tor and was heading deeper onto the moor. She and Charlie didn't know this area as well as they knew their own tor and the Riverdale wood.

Poppy almost jumped out of her skin when a long, black face loomed out of the mist. She stifled the urge to scream, realising with relief that it was one of the black-faced sheep that grazed the moor. The animal gave her a baleful stare before turning and running off into the bracken. She tried to steady her breathing. She knew she needed to stay calm.

The fog seemed more impenetrable than ever. What hope did a six-year-old have in this? Poppy tried not to think about life without her brother – it was inconceivable. She knew Caroline would be heartbroken if anything happened to Charlie. But instead of wallowing in jealousy, Poppy remembered Tory's advice and tried to see things through her stepmother's eyes. Charlie was the apple of his mum's eye but how did Caroline really feel about her? What must it have been like to take on someone else's child? Poppy knew she could be reserved and self-contained. Caroline had described her as prickly.

She'd been outraged at the time but knew deep down it was true. She'd always blamed her stepmother for not being Isobel. Caroline had tried so hard to break down the barriers Poppy had put up. Poppy wouldn't have blamed her if she'd thrown in the towel years ago. But she never had.

Was it too late, she wondered as she tramped on through the fog. Caroline had been so sad recently. Would she ever forgive Poppy if Charlie was hurt – or worse? Poppy started bargaining with herself. If she could bring her brother back safe and sound everything would be alright. She and Caroline could try again. But that was all well and good, she thought grimly, as she tripped over yet another slab of granite lying in her path. First she had to find him.

After walking for what seemed like hours with no sign of Charlie, Poppy was beginning to feel tearful. She could hear the catch in her throat when she tried shouting his name. The rain seemed fractionally lighter and Poppy tried to convince herself that the fog was beginning to clear. But she knew she was kidding herself. Maybe she should return to Riverdale and make sure Tory had called for help. Then she realised with a sinking feeling that she'd lost all sense of direction and had no idea how to get home. Exhaustion washed over her. She found a boulder and sat down while she tried to marshal her thoughts. Under its blanket of mist the moor was deathly quiet. Poppy slumped with her head in her hands, wondering what to do. She loved Dartmoor but today it seemed the creepiest, most dangerous place on earth. To make matters worse she couldn't shake the feeling that she was being watched.

She turned around slowly, hoping to see the face of another sheep and not a black panther on the prowl. Her heart hammered in her chest. Her eyes widened in shock as she saw two eyes staring intently at her through the mist.

CHAPTER 22

Poppy thought she must be hallucinating. She shook her head, swivelled round on the boulder and looked again, expecting to see nothing but fog. Not so. Standing about five metres away was the head of a ghost horse, looking straight at her. Cloud? No, it couldn't be. Poppy rubbed her eyes, but he was still there when she opened them. Squinting into the mist she could just make out the outline of his body. Not a phantom at all.

"Cloud!" Poppy whispered. She slid off the boulder and walked slowly up to him, her hand outstretched. He stood still, lowering his head as she came close, letting her stroke him.

Tears streamed down her cheeks.

"I can't find Charlie, Cloud. He's gone. I don't know what to do," she sobbed into his damp neck.

She felt him begin to move away from her. "Please don't leave me, Cloud. I'm so scared," she hiccupped through her tears. The pony stopped. She walked towards him, but as soon as she reached him he set off again, walking a few paces into the mist before stopping and turning to look at her. It was as if he wanted her to follow him.

After about half a mile Cloud came to a halt. Poppy stood next to him, her right hand resting lightly on his withers. In front of them was a sheer drop, a cliff of granite left by quarrymen two centuries earlier and now as much a part of the Dartmoor landscape as the tors that towered, unseen, above them. In the mist Poppy couldn't tell how deep the quarry was. She could hear Cloud breathing. She looked at him, hoping she wasn't about to send him galloping for the hills. She took a deep breath and yelled as loudly as she could.

"CHAR-LIE!"

The sound reverberated around the old quarry. Cloud stiffened beneath her hand, but didn't move. She called again, louder this time. As the echoes died away she thought she heard something. She called once more. This time she definitely heard an answering shout coming from the bottom of the quarry.

"Poppy! Is that you?"

"Charlie! I'm here! What happened? Are you OK?"

"I'm alright. I was looking for the big cat when I fell down this cliff. I haven't hurt myself but I couldn't climb back up again. I thought I might be here all night." His voice sounded ragged and Poppy felt her heart contract.

"Don't worry, I'm here now. And guess who helped me find you?"

"Was it Cloud? He was with me before. He came right up to me and I stroked his nose. I didn't find the big cat but I did find Cloud for you."

Poppy looked at the pony and then down into the quarry. Below her feet the rain-sodden grass gave way to a giant slab of granite which marked the edge of the quarry.

"Charlie, how far down did you fall, can you remember?" she called.

"Um. You know how high the roof of Chester's stable is?"

Poppy thought, that's not so bad.

"About four times as high as that."

Oh.

"But the bottom was more of a slope than a drop. I was doing my stuntman roll, otherwise I would've probably stopped sooner."

"Your stuntman roll?" she asked incredulously. Only Charlie could be thinking of stunts at a time like this.

"It's to stop you breaking any bones. You tuck up, then roll down the hill." Poppy could only assume her brother was giving a practical demonstration to the nearest sheep. But this wasn't getting them anywhere.

"Charlie, listen. I'm going to come down to get

you. I've got a couple of lead ropes to help get you up safely." She looked at Cloud again. His solid strength was so reassuring she couldn't face the thought of leaving him. It was probably the last chance she would have to catch him and return him to Riverdale before the drift. She couldn't bear the thought of him back at George Blackstone's farm. But she had to help Charlie.

Poppy clung to the pony's neck and whispered, "Stay safe, Cloud." He whickered softly and she reluctantly let him go. She took a couple of steps forward and sat on the edge of the quarry. She felt the unyielding stone beneath her as she turned onto her front and slithered down. For one terrifying moment she felt nothing but air beneath her feet as she dangled like a string puppet over the edge of the cliff. Her fingers curled around the root of an old gorse bush and she held on desperately while her feet struggled to find a foothold among the seams of granite.

"Poppy! Are you coming?" Charlie shouted from somewhere below.

"Yes. I'm on my way," she called back, resisting the urge to look down. Her feet found a crevice and she edged her way along it until she felt a slab of stone sticking out like a shelf. She stepped onto it gratefully. Her arms and legs felt like jelly and her fingers were numb.

"Not far now!" she called to her brother in a voice that sounded a lot braver than she felt. Once more she turned over and inched her way over the drop.

"I can see your wellies!" cried Charlie.

If Charlie could see her feet Poppy calculated that she couldn't have too far to fall. She took a deep breath and let go of the rock shelf, waiting for the ground to hit her. When she landed it was onto a gorse bush which ripped her waterproof coat. She felt its thorns tear her cheek as she tumbled onto the boggy grass beneath. Charlie ran up to her, appearing out of the fog like a tornado. He had painted his face with streaks of green and black and was wearing his camouflage trousers and a green waterproof coat. He would have been impossible to spot even on a clear day.

"Poppy!" He launched himself at her. She opened her arms and held him tightly. His face felt icy. He wriggled out of her grasp and looked at her, his blue eyes widening. "You're bleeding!"

"Am I?" She felt her cheek. It was wet. She looked at her scarlet hand and back at Charlie. "I'm fine," she answered. "But are you OK?"

"I ate the sausages I was going to use as bait for the big cat but they've made me really thirsty and I forgot to bring a drink. And I'm freezing. I think I'd like to go home now," he said. Together they looked up at the side of the quarry. The sheer granite looked as impenetrable as the walls of a castle. Poppy thought carefully. Even with the two lead ropes she doubted they would be able to climb even half way up the cliff. How on earth were they ever going to get out?

"Hold on a minute. Did you say Cloud came to you when you were down here?" she asked.

"Yes. He came so close I was able to stroke him. He wasn't frightened at all."

"There's no way Cloud could have made it down that drop. It means there must be another way out of the quarry." Poppy rubbed her cheek again and considered. "If this was a quarry they must have got the granite out somehow. I bet there's a path, maybe even an old railway track. We just need to find it."

Shivering, Charlie looked at his sister. "Maybe we could look for Cloud's hoofprints? They might show us the way."

"Yes, that's a good idea. Wait - I have a torch somewhere." She fished about in the pocket of her waterproof. "Here it is. I thought it might come in useful."

Together they searched for Cloud's hoofprints, using the beam of the torch to light the ground. But the peaty soil was so waterlogged it would have been impossible to make out the footprints of an elephant, let alone a pony.

Poppy began to lose hope that they'd ever find their way out.

"I'm so tired. Can't we find somewhere to sit down for a while? Just until the sun comes out?" Charlie wheedled. Poppy knew she had to keep her brother moving. She took his hand. His teeth had started to chatter.

"You're freezing. Take my coat, that'll warm you

up a bit. Let's sing a song to keep us going. You choose." And so to Ten in a Bed they carried on tramping through the fog away from the granite cliff-face. Occasionally a startled sheep would leap out of their path and once they heard the plaintiff caw of a rook flying overhead. Progress was slow. Charlie, normally so full of bounce, was lethargic. Every now and then he would plead with her to stop for a rest. Finally she relented and they found a boulder to perch on.

"Just for five minutes," she told him firmly, wrapping her arm around him in an attempt to keep him warm. "I wonder if the search and rescue people are out looking for us," she thought out loud. "Maybe they're only minutes away. I expect they have one of those big St Bernard dogs with them with a barrel around his collar filled with chocolate." She attempted a smile.

"Do you think they might be? I hope so. I miss Mum."

"So do I," said Poppy, knowing it was true.

"Do you think we'll ever get home?" he asked sleepily.

Poppy gave her brother a squeeze. "Of course we will. I promised Mum I'd look after you, didn't I?" She'd tried the word experimentally. It didn't sound as awkward as she'd thought it might. A few minutes later, as she rubbed her hands together in a feeble attempt to warm her freezing fingers, she noticed his head droop forward.

"Charlie!" she said urgently. "Don't fall asleep. We need to keep moving." She pulled him to a standing position and held onto him as he started swaying. She took his hand and they stumbled on through the fog. Then suddenly she stopped.

"Wait a minute. Isn't this the rock we had our picnic on? We can't be far from Riverdale."

Charlie, still shivering, shrugged his shoulders. He looked utterly defeated. "I don't want to walk any more. I just want to go to sleep," he whined, his bottom lip wobbling.

Feeling increasingly desperate Poppy tried to adopt Caroline's calm manner. "Charlie, we are nearly home, I promise. Just a little bit further, then you can go to bed with a lovely hot water bottle. Think how nice that'll be."

A cry pierced the gloom but Poppy dismissed it as another rook, wheeling overhead. They continued trudging wearily on. But the call was followed by another, louder this time. Poppy listened hard with blood pounding in her head, her senses on full alert. Please let it be help, she thought. For Charlie's sake.

CHAPTER 23

Inspector Bill Pearson dunked a digestive biscuit into his mug of tea as he studied a map of Dartmoor, which had been hastily blue-tacked to the wall directly opposite him. Usually the room, on the top floor of the police station, was where officers kept their kit in lockers and spent their breaks microwaving meals and watching sport on a flat screen in the corner. Today the television was silent. The room had been set up as an incident room, a nerve centre where the police were co-ordinating the search for the two missing children.

The 999 call to say the brother and sister had disappeared from their home near Waterby had come in to the force control room at just before eleven o'clock that morning.

The children had now been missing for two hours

and, with the weather on the moor deteriorating by the minute, the search for them was being treated as a critical incident.

Inspector Pearson had been put in charge of the search by his chief inspector and was expecting a long shift. He was due to go home at four o'clock but with two children missing on the moor in weather like this he knew the odds of finishing on time were long, to say the least.

Ignoring the buttons straining across his large stomach he reached for another biscuit.

"How many have we got on the moor now, Woody?" he asked the man sitting next to him.

Sergeant Wood was as thin as Inspector Pearson was round. He looked disapprovingly at his superior as the inspector took a large bite of the soggy digestive.

"Well, boss. We have all our available late shift officers and three Dartmoor search and rescue teams on the moor, two of them with dogs. They're searching a three mile radius of the house, although they're looking to extend that if we haven't found the children before it gets dark."

"What about the chopper? Surely the thermal imaging camera's going to be our best bet?" asked the inspector.

"The helicopter's grounded because of the fog, boss. The search is going to have to be done on foot."

"That's going to make things tough. What do we

know about the two children?"

"They were being looked after by a friend of the family who has been staying with them while their mother's in hospital. Mrs McKeever broke her wrist yesterday, by all accounts, but is due home this afternoon."

"They're not having a very good week, are they?" remarked Inspector Pearson.

"The boy, Charlie, left the house some time before ten this morning. He's six. According to the family friend his sister Poppy, who's eleven, discovered her brother had gone walkabout and went looking for him on her own. We think she's been missing since about half past ten."

Inspector Pearson looked at the clock. One o'clock. The rain was still drumming against the window. Dartmoor was no place for children on a day like this.

"What about a media appeal?"

"We're working on that, guv. The on call press officer has been briefed. We're just waiting for the go-ahead from the mother. Then we'll get someone down to the house to pick up some recent photos of the kids."

"Do we have someone at hospital with the mother?" he asked.

"Yes, boss. PC Bodiam has been there since about half past eleven."

Inspector Pearson looked at the map again. By Dartmoor standards Riverdale wasn't particularly remote, but it edged on to an isolated part of the moor where the terrain could be dangerous. Add to that the worsening weather. The temperatures plummeted at night at this time of year. If the children weren't found before nightfall they didn't stand a chance, he thought grimly.

The next couple of hours passed quickly in the makeshift incident room. Every half an hour briefings were given and the inspector updated on the progress of the search. More cups of tea were made and more digestive biscuits were dunked. North east of Riverdale police officers and volunteers from the Dartmoor Rescue Group, in their trademark red jackets, scoured the landscape for any trace of the two children. At just after three o'clock hopes were raised when one of the trained search dogs found a small digital camera. The information was radioed to PC Claire Bodiam at Tavistock Hospital who asked Caroline McKeever if either of the children had a camera, and if so, what make and model.

"Yes," Caroline replied quietly. "I bought Charlie his own digital camera for Christmas last year so he could take his wildlife pictures on it. It's a Canon, although I have no idea what model it is. But it's silver, if that's any help."

PC Bodiam nodded and relayed the message back to the incident room. She smiled reassuringly at Caroline, who was white with worry.

"It looks as if it is Charlie's camera they've found," she confirmed. Seeing the fear on Caroline's face PC

Bodiam tried to set her mind at rest. "It's good news, Mrs McKeever. It means the search teams are definitely in the right area. I'm sure it won't be long before we find Poppy and Charlie."

But another hour passed and there was still no sign of the children. Back in the incident room Inspector Pearson was about to incur the wrath of his wife by texting her to say he would be late home. Just as he started tapping out the message his radio crackled. He held it to his ear. Over the airwaves a voice shouted, "We've found them, guv!" He deleted the text message with relief. "Are they alright?" he asked.

"The lad is showing early signs of hypothermia and will need to go to hospital. We've just radioed for an ambulance. The girl is fine," replied the police officer who had been leading the search teams up on the moor.

"Good job. Has anyone let the mother know?"

"PC Bodiam is next on my list to call, guv."

Inspector Pearson was puzzled. "What on earth possessed the children to do a disappearing act on the moor in this weather?" he asked.

"They'd gone looking for big cats apparently, guv," the radio crackled.

The inspector raised his eyebrows. "I might have known. Sniffer Smith was on to the press office a couple of days ago asking for a police comment on a sighting of the so-called Beast of Dartmoor. For something that doesn't even exist, that damn creature has a lot to answer for."

CHAPTER 24

Poppy couldn't stop shivering. Tory sat her down in front of the fire in the lounge and wrapped her in her duvet to warm her up, but her body refused to stop trembling. Charlie, who was bundled up in his Thomas the Tank Engine duvet next to her, was trying to sip a mug of hot chocolate through chattering teeth. Tory, watching them anxiously, said, "It's probably the shock. You'll both be as right as rain after a good night's sleep."

Henry Blossom stood by the window, keeping an eye out for the lights of the ambulance. Poppy could hear the quiet murmur of chat coming from the kitchen, where the two remaining members of the police search team were making cups of tea. She'd been surprised to see Henry when they'd finally arrived back at Riverdale, exhausted and chilled to the bone. "He was the first person I called when I realised you and Charlie had gone. I didn't want to phone the police straight away in case you were both tucked up in one of the outbuildings, or had gone up to the farm together. Henry searched the grounds for me while I went over the house. That's when I found Charlie's note, realised what must have happened and called the police," Tory had explained.

Her grey hair was mussed up as though she'd spent all day running her hands through it in worry. But her brown eyes were as kind as ever.

"I'm truly sorry for disappearing without telling you and causing everyone such trouble," Poppy said for about the tenth time that afternoon.

"It's alright, pet. I know you were worried about Charlie. At least you're both safe. All's well that ends well. That's what my old mum used to say."

"My mum had another saying," smiled Henry from his post by the window. "What doesn't kill you makes you stronger. Oh look, here's the ambulance at last."

Charlie was so tired he could barely keep his eyes open but rallied when he heard that it had finally arrived.

"Cool! My first ride in an ambulance! Though I've been to the hospital near our old house loads of times," he informed Henry proudly. "Do you think they'll use the lights and sirens?"

"They only use blues and twos for emergencies I'm afraid, Charlie," Henry replied, glad to see the six-year-old smiling again. Both children had been subdued since they'd been home and looked lost without Caroline. He was glad they'd soon be reunited with her at the hospital in Tavistock.

Tory was allowed to ride with them in the back of the ambulance and Charlie spent the half hour journey in heaven being shown defibrillators, spine boards, inflatable splints and the burns kit. Poppy chatted quietly to Tory, describing how Cloud had found her in the fog and led her to Charlie.

"I probably could have caught Cloud but I was so worried about Charlie – I had to put him first," said Poppy, her eyes downcast.

"You did the right thing, pet," said Tory, patting her gently on the knee. "Cloud has run wild on the moor for years, he can look after himself. Look how clever he was today, leading you to Charlie. He'll be fine, I know he will." Poppy attempted a smile and tried to believe her.

Before long they drew up outside the hospital and the two paramedics helped them down the ambulance steps and into the minor injury unit where Caroline was waiting for them, her arms outstretched, a look of pure relief on her face. Charlie was usually quick to rush into his mother's arms but this time Poppy beat him to it.

"Thank God," Caroline murmured into Poppy's hair as Charlie joined in the hug, Caroline gingerly holding her broken wrist above his head. "I've been so worried about you both. You two mean the world to me, you do know that, don't you?"

Poppy looked into her stepmother's blue eyes and nodded. "Yes, I do. And I'm sorry - for everything."

"What do you mean? If you hadn't gone after Charlie God knows what would have happened to him up on the moor on a day like today. You saved his life, Poppy."

"I didn't mean for today. I'm sorry for the last six years. For everything."

"Shhh. It's all forgotten. I think today is the perfect day to start all over again, don't you?"

Poppy nodded gratefully and smiled at her stepmother, who hugged her again.

Charlie broke the silence. "Is Dad coming home?"

"He's tried to get permission from his newsdesk to come home early and they've said they'll do all they can but we don't know when he'll be back I'm afraid, sweetheart. I've managed to get a message to him that you're both OK and he sends his love," Caroline replied, and, realising a doctor was hovering in the background, let the children go.

Once they'd been checked over and declared fit to return home Tory called Henry Blossom, who had volunteered to drive the four of them back to Riverdale.

"I've got an idea," Caroline said, with a twinkle in her eye. "Shall we stop off on the way and treat ourselves to a fish and chip supper?"

"Oh, yes please!" shouted Charlie. "This has been the best day ever! I get to meet loads of real live police, stroke two proper search dogs, ride in an ambulance *and* have fish and chips for tea. It's been awesome!"

The three adults and Poppy exchanged looks before bursting out laughing. Charlie scratched his head and looked at them. "Did I say something funny?"

CHAPTER 25

They were just finishing their fish and chips when there was a thump on the back door.

"It's only me!" yelled Scarlett. "I'm back from Granny's and wanted to talk to Poppy about school."

Scarlett stood stock still as she took in the presence of Tory and Henry Blossom and noticed Caroline's broken wrist.

"Well, you've obviously had a much more exciting week than me," she commented. "Granny's was sooo boring. She thinks cross stitch is an exciting hobby and her television stopped working when they went over to digital. We spent most of the time visiting ancient aunties and looking around stately homes. It's been gruesome. I'm so glad to be home, even if we do start Year Seven tomorrow."

Poppy swallowed. She'd pushed all thoughts of

secondary school to the back of her mind but now it was just hours away. She looked at Caroline. "Is it OK if we chill out in my room for a bit so I can fill Scarlett in on all the dramas?"

"Of course, sweetheart. I'm going to get Charlie to bed and then crash in front of the television. Henry's taking Tory home."

The two girls dashed upstairs to Poppy's room. Caroline had already pulled the curtains, laid out clean pyjamas and switched on the fairy lights, which twinkled merrily over Poppy's bed. Scarlett sat on the wicker chair by the window. "Right. I want to hear *everything*," she said.

Twenty minutes later Poppy had brought her friend up to speed. "I wish I'd been here to help," Scarlett said fervently.

"So do I," said Poppy. "I was terrified something had happened to Charlie. And I feel so guilty about leaving Cloud. If it wasn't for him we'd probably still be on the moor. I can't stop thinking about it."

"The drift is two weeks away. There's still time to catch him," Scarlett pointed out. "Anyway, I'd better make a move. Mum only let me come if I promised I wouldn't be longer than half an hour. Are you all ready for the morning?"

"Yes, my uniform, PE kit and new shoes are in the wardrobe. I just need to sort out my rucksack." Poppy went quiet. She knew Scarlett wouldn't judge her. "Actually, I'm dreading it," she admitted.

"Don't worry. We'll stick together and I'll

introduce you to the girls from my primary school. A few of them are lame but most of them are really nice. You'll be fine. Don't forget, the bus goes from the bottom of the lane at ten to eight. So let's meet at the postbox at twenty to and we'll walk down together. Mum's told Alex he's got to look after us. He's over the moon, as you can imagine," Scarlett giggled.

When Scarlett had gone Poppy lay on her bed staring at the ceiling and wishing she was as sociable and outgoing as her friend. Caroline stuck her head around the bedroom door.

"Pat's just phoned to say she'll take Charlie to and from school for me until I can drive again. Isn't that kind of her?"

Poppy nodded. "And Scarlett and I are going to walk to the bus stop together in the morning."

"That's a good idea. Why don't you come down and say goodbye to Tory and Henry and I'll run you a nice hot bath. You mustn't be too late to bed tonight."

Poppy felt as though she'd been asleep for a nano second when her Mickey Mouse alarm clock woke her with a shrill ring the next morning. She threw off the duvet, jumped out of bed and looked out of the window. The day before the tor had been completely concealed by fog. This morning it was bathed in mellow autumn sunshine.

Downstairs in the kitchen Caroline was singing. She broke off when Poppy walked in. "How are you feeling, sweetheart?" she asked, her blue eyes full of concern.

"Much better, thanks. I finally feel warm again," Poppy said, reaching for a box of cereal.

"Good. Charlie's still in bed. I thought I'd let him lie in."

Poppy raised her eyebrows. "Are you sure? That's what I thought yesterday and he turned out to be your dressing gown."

"No, he definitely is. I heard him snoring. Unless he's invented a snoring sound effect and is now halfway across Dartmoor looking for his wretched panther."

"I wouldn't put it past him," said Poppy. She caught Caroline's eye and they started giggling. The giggles bubbled into laughter and soon they were both laughing hysterically at the thought of Charlie rigging up a snoring soundtrack before creeping, SAS style, back onto the moor.

"As your dad's not here perhaps he had to make do with recording Magpie snoring," snorted Caroline, wiping tears from her eyes.

Poppy clutched her stomach and dissolved into giggles again. Her dad could snore for England. She tried taking deep breaths but every time she looked at Caroline they broke into peels of laughter. Poppy remembered the day Scarlett had made Caroline chuckle with stories of school and how jealous she'd been, watching from the sidelines. It felt so good to laugh with her stepmother. She realised that the only person leaving her out of everything had been herself.

Before she knew it she was walking reluctantly down the Riverdale drive in her new school uniform. The navy blazer felt scratchy around her neck and her new shoes rubbed her ankles uncomfortably. Poppy had worn polo shirts at primary school and after their fit of the giggles Caroline had shown her how to knot her new navy and gold striped tie.

"If you can do a quick release knot you'll soon get the hang of this. You look so grown up, Poppy. Let me take a photo so I can email it to your dad. He'll be so sad he's missed your first day at secondary school."

The bus ride into Tavistock was nerve-wracking and even Scarlett seemed intimidated by the too-cool-for-school sixth-formers, even though she could vaguely remember some of them from her primary school. In a whisper Scarlett filled Poppy in on everyone's family histories so that by the time the bus pulled into the layby outside their new school she knew whose great aunt had married her first cousin and whose dad had been arrested for sheep rustling.

In fact the day Poppy had been dreading for weeks whizzed by. The two girls were delighted to discover they were in the same form but horrified when they were given their fortnightly timetables, which contained tortures like double science and maths. Their form teacher was a tall, thin, anxious-looking man called Mr Herbert. Some of the boys had already nicknamed him Filthy. Scarlett introduced Poppy to her friends from primary school and the girls trailed around endless corridors searching for the right classrooms whenever the bell went. There was a certain camaraderie among the new Year Sevens. They'd spent the last year strutting around their primary schools with all the confidence of very big fish in very small ponds. Suddenly everyone, even the most self-assured among them, felt as insignificant as sprats, back at the bottom of the pecking order.

At lunchtime Alex came to find them to check they were OK. Being in Year Nine gave him a certain amount of kudos and a couple of the Year Seven girls sitting near them tittered nervously as he chatted to Scarlett and Poppy about their morning.

"Scarlett, is that really your brother? He's so good-looking," said one dreamily as Alex walked away.

"You're joking, right? You don't have to live with him and his sweaty trainers. He's a complete and utter pain in the –". At that moment the bell went and they gathered up their lunchboxes and trundled slowly out of the canteen in a river of navy blue and burgundy.

By Thursday Poppy and Scarlett were beginning to find their way around the school and were getting to know more of their classmates. Charlie had started at Scarlett's old primary school the previous day and had already made firm friends with a boy called Ed, whose dad was the local farrier. The evenings were getting darker and Poppy had at least an hour's homework every night. She hadn't had a chance to see Cloud all week and fretted about him constantly.

On Friday the Tavistock Herald published its story

about Charlie's big cat sighting alongside a shorter article about the search operation for two children who had gone missing on the moor the previous weekend. Charlie produced the paper with a flourish the minute Poppy let herself in the back door after school. She flung her rucksack under the kitchen table and settled down to read. The big cat story took up most of page three. Next to Charlie's picture of the cat were Henry Blossom's photo of Charlie and Poppy and a file picture of a black panther with the caption, *Could a creature like this be roaming Dartmoor?*

Exclusive: Boy captures Beast of Dartmoor on camera
By Stanley Smith

A six-year-old Waterby boy has astounded big cat experts after capturing the clearest photo yet of the so-called Beast of Dartmoor.

Charlie McKeever was with his 11-year-old sister Poppy on the moor near Waterby last Thursday when they saw the black panther-like creature.

"The cat was massive and we were both absolutely terrified," *said Charlie, whose dad Mike McKeever is one of the BBC's top war correspondents.*

"We weren't terrified," said Poppy indignantly.

"I know. Sniffer Smith seems to have embellished most of the quotes," Caroline replied drily. Poppy continued reading.

The quick-thinking Waterby Primary School pupil grabbed his digital camera and took this photograph seconds before the cat leapt from the boulder and disappeared onto the moor.

Big cat enthusiast John Clancy, who has been tracking the fabled Beast of Dartmoor for the last five years, said the image was irrefutable evidence that the big cat existed.

"Thanks to a brave six-year-old we can at last prove to the sceptics that there is a black panther living on our doorstep," he added.

But Tavistock Police Inspector Bill Pearson was quick to dismiss the sighting. He told the Herald: "I really don't know why people continue to get so excited about the so-called Beast of Dartmoor. Call me cynical but it's probably just someone's overweight black moggie that's strayed too far from home."

Have you seen the Beast of Dartmoor? We'd love to hear your story. Email the newsroom now.

"We're famous, Poppy!" said Charlie. "Everyone at school's going to think we're so cool."

Poppy quickly scanned the second article about the search and rescue operation. Inspector Pearson was quoted as saying he was glad the outcome had been a happy one while issuing a stern warning about the dangers of Dartmoor. He hadn't released their names to the press and she was relieved to see that Sniffer hadn't made the connection. But her name was still plastered all over the local paper. She hated the limelight and couldn't imagine anything worse than being the centre of attention, especially at school. The very suggestion made her feel sick.

Seeing her concern Caroline squeezed Poppy's hand. "Don't worry, sweetheart. By Monday people will be wrapping their fish and chips and lining their cat litter trays with the Herald. It'll be old news. Now, what would you like for tea?"

CHAPTER 26

Poppy's head was filled with thoughts of Cloud when she awoke the next morning. The drift was exactly a week away and she knew the weekend would be her last chance to catch him and bring him home to Riverdale. She picked up her mobile phone from the bedside table and texted Scarlett.

Hi Scar, any chance we can go for a ride on the moor and see if we can find you know who? P x

The screen flashed with a reply within seconds.

Course. Be here for ten. I'll be by the stables. C U later! S ;-)

Poppy hadn't ridden for a couple of weeks and it felt great to be back in the saddle. Flynn seemed as pleased to be out as she was and looked around with his bay ears pricked as they followed Scarlett and Blaze along the rocky track that led from Ashworthy to the moor. Scarlett chattered about school while Poppy scanned the horizon looking for Cloud's dappled grey coat. They headed towards the Riverdale tor and as they drew nearer were bemused to see a huddle of people at the foot of the tor, looking and pointing to the cairn at the top.

"Who on earth are they?" cried Poppy. "Cloud's not going to come near with that lot hanging around."

Scarlett swung around in her saddle to get a better look. The group was mainly middle-aged men with cameras around their necks. A couple were filming with camcorders.

"Do you know what, I think they've probably come to look for Charlie's black panther," she told her friend. "I expect they read the story in yesterday's Herald."

Poppy's heart sank. "Typical. We might as well give up now. Cloud will be miles away."

"Let's at least ride over to Riverdale wood and see if he's there. You never know," said Scarlett. But although they saw a couple of small herds of Dartmoor ponies there was no sign of Cloud.

It was the same story the next day. Even more people had turned up hoping to get a glimpse of the famous Beast of Dartmoor. Poppy felt so frustrated she could have wept. With school the next day she knew that any chance she had of saving Cloud from the drift had all but disappeared.

Caroline sensed her despair as they sat down to roast chicken that evening. She waited until Charlie had gone to bed before she tackled Poppy.

"Something's up, I know it is. Are you worried about school tomorrow?"

"No, it's not that," Poppy replied miserably.

"You know you can tell me anything, don't you Poppy? I'm on your side."

Poppy looked at Caroline across the kitchen table and managed a weak smile. "I know you are. I should have told you sooner. I don't really know why I didn't. But I don't want to keep secrets from you any more."

Over the next half an hour Caroline listened quietly as Poppy told her about Cloud. How she'd glimpsed the flash of white in the woods they day they moved to Riverdale and the first time she and Charlie saw him by the river. She recounted how her suspicions that Tory knew where the pony had come from had been correct. Caroline looked shocked when Poppy described the hunter trial where Cloud had fallen in the mud, trapping Caitlyn beneath him, and how the pony had ended up at George Blackstone's farm before being set free by a heartbroken Tory.

"You know Charlie and I kept going to watch the badgers? We weren't. We were out looking for Cloud," said Poppy, not daring to meet her stepmother's eyes. "Every year Tory used Chester to lead Cloud to Riverdale where she kept him in the stable hidden from the drift," she continued. "That's what I was going to do last Sunday when you were in hospital. I had everything planned. Then Charlie went missing and I knew I had to go looking for him instead. But Cloud found me in the fog and led me to Charlie. It's Cloud who saved Charlie, not me."

When she finally raised her eyes to Caroline's face she could see only concern so she ploughed on. "And the drift is next Saturday, so I'm too late to save Cloud now."

Caroline looked at her stepdaughter. Poppy's shoulders were slumped and her green eyes were forlorn.

"Oh Poppy, I had no idea. I could have helped, you know. You may not believe it but I was as pony-mad as you when I was your age."

"You never said."

"You never asked, sweetheart," Caroline replied. "And I was lucky enough to have my own pony. I didn't like to rub your nose in it."

"What was your pony like?" Poppy asked.

Caroline's face took on a faraway look. "His name was Hamilton and he was a fleabitten grey, not dappled like your Cloud. He was 14.2hh and the love of my life." She looked at Poppy and smiled. "You go and sit by the fire. I'll be with you in a minute."

The lounge was warm and cosy and although she couldn't shake the wretchedness she'd felt all weekend Poppy felt glad to be cocooned inside after the strain of the last few days. Caroline re-appeared with a tatty old shoebox tied up with a faded red ribbon. She sat down on the sofa beside Poppy and attempted to open the box one-handed.

"Let me help," said Poppy. "What's inside?" she asked as she leant in to get a closer look.

"Just some photographs I thought you might like to see."

Photo after photo showed a handsome grey pony, ears pricked as he looked over his stable door, caked in mud while he grazed in his field, pulling hay from a net tied to a five bar gate. She riffled through the pictures. There were photos of the pony jumping over small fences, being shampooed, having his mane plaited and new shoes fitted.

"Is that you?" Poppy asked Caroline, pointing to a photograph of the pony nuzzling the ear of a slim blonde girl about Poppy's age.

"Yes. And that's Hamilton. I think I was about twelve when that photo was taken. You can see his stable in the background."

"He was beautiful. He reminds me a bit of Cloud," said Poppy, a catch in her voice.

"He was. And he was such fun. We had a ball together, we really did. For three years he was the most important thing in my life."

"What happened to him?" Poppy asked.

"You remember my dad used to work for an oil company before he retired?" Poppy nodded. "When I was fourteen he was posted overseas and your Auntie Lizzie and I were sent to boarding school. My parents said we had to sell Hamilton. He went to a nice family but I was absolutely devastated. I never rode again."

Poppy reached over and gave her stepmother a

hug. Caroline held her close. "I really do understand how you feel," she said, wiping a tear from Poppy's cheek.

"I know you do. It's just so unfair. I know something awful will happen to Cloud and there's nothing I can do to help him. He trusted me, I know he did. And I've let him down."

"Don't give up hope, Poppy. We'll go out early on the morning of the drift. You never know – you still have time to bring him home to Riverdale."

Poppy seriously doubted it, but she supposed there was at least a chance. She tucked her legs up and sank back into the sofa, resting her head on Caroline's shoulder.

"I'm glad I've told you about Cloud," she mumbled.

Caroline kissed the top of her head. "So am I, sweetheart. So am I."

CHAPTER 27

"Dad phoned after you went to bed last night," Caroline informed the two children at breakfast the next day. "His newsdesk has finally agreed to send in another correspondent to replace him. He's flying out on Saturday night and should be home some time on Sunday."

"Hurray!" shouted Charlie, his mouth smeared with raspberry jam. "Did you tell him I'm headline news?"

"No, not yet!" Caroline laughed. "I thought you'd want to tell him yourself."

Caroline looked happier than she had for weeks, Poppy thought as she shrugged on her blazer and let herself out of the back door. Scarlett was waiting for her by the postbox and as they walked to the bus stop together Poppy realised with surprise that she was actually looking forward to school. A couple of her new classmates gave her some gentle ribbing about the story in the Herald but she followed Scarlett's advice and played along with them and her five minutes of fame were soon forgotten.

At lunchtime their talk inevitably turned to Cloud and the drift. It was all Poppy thought about these days.

"I'm going try one last time to find Cloud before they start rounding up the ponies on Saturday morning. Caroline's going to come with me," she told her friend.

"I don't believe it," groaned Scarlett. "Mum's dragging me and Alex to Plymouth for the day on Saturday. Says we both need new clothes for the winter. There's no way she'll let me come with you instead. Normally I'd love a day's shopping but I'd much rather help you catch Cloud."

Privately Poppy thought that the fewer people who were looking for Cloud the better, but hurting her friend's feelings was the last thing she wanted to do so she grimaced convincingly and said, "That's such a shame. But I promise I'll text you if we do find him."

Saturday morning finally arrived, mild and sunny. By nine o'clock Poppy, Charlie and Caroline were ready to go. Poppy ran into the tackroom, grabbed an old rucksack and swung it over her shoulders before looking over the door of Chester's stable.

"I'm keeping you in today," she told the old donkey. "I don't want you being upset by all the noise and commotion of the drift. You'll be safe in here."

She blew him a kiss and joined Caroline and Charlie. They set off towards Waterby, where the ponies would be herded into a temporary corral before they were sorted. As they walked they could hear the distant sound of neighing and the roar of quad bikes. Poppy could feel her stomach churning. They passed flat-capped farmers in checked shirts and tweed jackets, their craggy faces inscrutable as they headed for the moors, walking sticks in hand.

"Scarlett said that some of the people rounding up the ponies are on horseback and others ride quad bikes," said Poppy, slightly out of breath as they marched up a steep lane that led to one of the bigger tors behind Waterby.

"Look!" cried Charlie, as they rounded a corner and the moor stretched out in front of them. In the distance they could see a small group of Dartmoor ponies picking their way through the rocks as they headed towards the village. The herd, driven by three women on cobs and a boy in his late teens on a quad bike, was soon joined by another gaggle of ponies that cantered down a grassy path flanked by gorse bushes. Their coats already thickening in preparation for a harsh Dartmoor winter, the ponies flashed past Poppy, Caroline and Charlie. Poppy's eyes skimmed the dark bays, blacks, chestnuts, skewbalds, piebalds and red and blue roans. There were two grey ponies in the group, but neither was Cloud and she breathed a sigh of relief.

For the next couple of hours they watched as more

and more ponies trickled down from the highest parts of the moor, forming a mass of streaming manes and heaving flanks. There was still no sign of Cloud and Poppy could feel her spirits rise. He knew the moor so well. Maybe he had managed to hide from the drivers.

"Well, hello!" said a familiar voice, and the three of them turned to see Henry Blossom standing behind them, his camera around his neck, his camera bag attached, as always, to his stooped right shoulder.

"How are you all? Not planning another adventure on the moor I hope?" he asked, looking at Charlie with a grin.

"No," answered Charlie, sheepishly. "We're watching the ponies. Why are you here?"

"I'm covering the drift for the Herald – we do every year," he explained. He looked behind to where Sniffer Smith, notebook in hand, was talking to one of the rugged old farmers. "This year Sniffer is planning to write a feature and flog it to one of the Sunday papers. Always has his eye on the main chance, that one."

Poppy glanced at the journalist, who was now heading towards them. Sniffer was as unpleasant as Henry was likeable, and she didn't trust him one inch.

"Shall we go?" she said under her breath to Caroline who, seeing Sniffer approaching, agreed at once. They said hasty goodbyes to Henry before turning and walking off.

"What do you want to do now, Poppy? Stay and

watch the ponies as they come off the moor to see if we see Cloud?" asked Caroline.

"If I was Cloud I'd be hiding in the Riverdale wood," announced Charlie suddenly. "It's so overgrown the quad bikes and horses and riders wouldn't be able to get in. We could go and have a look."

"That's actually a really good idea, Charlie. If we walk quickly it shouldn't take us more than half an hour to get there," said Poppy.

"But what are we going to do if we do see him?" Caroline asked.

Poppy looked over her shoulder at her rucksack. "I've got a headcollar and leadrope in here, plus a scoop filled with Chester's pony nuts. It's been digging in my back all morning. I just hope Cloud trusts me enough to let me catch him."

Half an hour later they reached the edge of the wood. Caroline followed the two children as they plunged into the trees, struggling to keep up as they ducked and weaved around branches and over fallen logs.

"You seem to know the wood pretty well," she panted, as they all stopped in front of a fallen tree trunk.

"Must be all that badger watching," grinned Poppy, as she scrambled over, Charlie following closely behind. Eventually they reached the river and followed it down to the small beach where Poppy and Charlie had first seen Cloud. There was no sign of him today.

"What should we do, Poppy?" asked Caroline quietly.

"I think you and Charlie should go and sit on that log and I'll stay here by the river with the pony nuts and headcollar. I've a feeling Cloud will come to us."

"How can you be so sure?"

Poppy's green eyes were shining. "Because I'm pretty certain that for the last ten minutes he's been following us."

CHAPTER 28

Poppy's conviction that Cloud was nearby started to waver when he didn't immediately appear from behind the trees. When he still hadn't showed after another ten minutes the fleeting elation she'd felt drained away to be replaced once again by nerves. Caroline gave her an encouraging smile from the log where she was stationed with Charlie. Poppy could see her brother was getting fidgety. Any minute now he'd realise he was hungry and then it would only be a matter of time before they had to abandon their rescue mission and head back home.

Just as she was about to admit defeat she heard the branches behind her rustle. Spinning around she almost cried out with relief when she saw Cloud's familiar grey nose poking out from behind the russet and gold leaves of a beech tree. She looked over at

Caroline and Charlie, pressing her finger to her lips. Charlie gave her the thumbs up and she could see Caroline crossing her fingers for luck.

Poppy started talking softly to Cloud, hoping he wouldn't sense the nerves that were making her voice wobble. He emerged slowly from the trees and at once she could see that something was very wrong. His flanks were dark with sweat and he was trembling with fear. Yet he looked straight at her, his brown eyes locked on hers, as she held out the scoop filled with pony nuts. As he approached she realised with shock that Cloud was now so lame he couldn't put any weight on his near hind leg.

"You poor, poor pony. What's happened to you? Did you get caught up in the drift?" she crooned softly as he hobbled towards her. Still talking, she stretched out her arm. Cloud hesitated and Poppy thought for a moment that she'd lost him. But then, as if he'd made up his mind to trust her, he whickered, walked forward and started eating the nuts.

Poppy ran her hand along his neck and he leaned into her. She put the scoop on the floor and with one hand on Cloud's neck slowly reached for the headcollar by her feet with the other. She put the leadrope around his neck while keeping up her monologue. Her fingers were shaking and she fumbled trying to undo the buckle of the headcollar. She glanced over at Caroline and Charlie, who were watching intently. The pounding in her ears almost drowned out the constant background rumble of quad bikes and neighing horses.

The buckle now undone, Poppy slowly edged the noseband over Cloud's muzzle. His ears twitched back and forth but he didn't pull away and as she pulled the strap over his poll with her left hand she felt a surge of triumph.

But just as she started to do up the buckle an explosion, as loud as the crack of a gunshot, pierced the air. Poppy jumped out of her skin, letting go of the headcollar, which slithered to the floor by her feet. Cloud half-reared in fright, turned in mid-air and fled back into the trees. Poppy sank to her knees, her head in her hands. Caroline and Charlie rushed over and Poppy felt Caroline's arm around her shoulders.

"What was it?" she cried, tears running down her cheeks.

"It sounded like a quad bike backfiring. I'm so sorry, Poppy, but Cloud's gone," said Caroline.

"That's it, then," Poppy said, blinking back the tears. "It's all my fault. I dropped the headcollar and now he's going to get caught. I've failed him."

"Don't say that, sweetheart. It's not your fault. No-one could have done any more than you." Caroline held out her arms. "Come here."

Poppy's legs felt like jelly but she stood up and went to Caroline and they clung together, Poppy's head tucked under Caroline's chin, until Charlie started grumbling that he was starving.

Caroline stroked Poppy's hair, lifted her chin and

looked directly at her. "Don't give up hope, angel. I know it doesn't feel like it now, but these things have a habit of working out in the end, you'll see."

Once Poppy would have let rip, accusing her stepmother of not understanding or getting it all wrong as usual. But things had changed   she no longer felt angry with Caroline. Instead she nodded mutely, misery descending as she thought how Cloud, with his poor damaged leg, would never escape being caught now.

"Would you like to see the last of the drift?" Caroline asked gently.

"No," Poppy replied. "I think I'd just like to go home."

Half a mile away the last few stragglers were being rounded up by two men on quad bikes. A small herd of ponies, led by an old bay stallion who had witnessed countless drifts during his long life on the moor, had been discovered grazing on the edge of the Riverdale wood. The herd, half a dozen mares and their yearlings and foals, followed the stallion, delicately picking a path through the gorse and bracken that marked the end of the wood and the beginning of the moor.

"I think this is probably the last of them," shouted one of the quad bike riders, a middle-aged man whose close-cropped hair was flecked with grey.

His younger companion was about to agree when he saw another pony emerge from the wood. "Hold on - look what the cat's just dragged in!"

The two men stopped revving their bikes and watched a dappled grey pony approach. He was limping badly, his head nodding in pain every time he took a step. His flanks were dark with sweat and his mane and tail were matted.

"Good grief!" exclaimed the older man. "He's in a sorry state. I'm not sure he's going to keep up with the rest of them. We might have to take it slowly."

One of the mares whinnied and Cloud whickered in return. "He's not a Dartmoor pony but they seem to know him alright," said the younger rider.

"I wonder –" mused his companion. A couple of years ago, over a pint of beer, one of the old farm hands had told him about the Connemara pony that had killed Tory Wickens' granddaughter at a local hunter trial. The pony had never been caught in the annual drift. Everyone had assumed it must have died during one of Dartmoor's unforgiving winters. Apparently not.

The younger rider, itching to get home, started revving his bike and the grey pony hobbled over to join the rest of the herd.

"Come on! We'll be here all night unless we get a move on," he yelled. The older man nodded. He turned his quad bike and started driving the ponies towards Waterby. Although the grey pony was now surrounded by the herd he stuck out like a sore thumb. He stood a couple of hands higher than the native ponies and was obviously of a much finer build. He had a noble look about him.

The quad bike rider had the distinct feeling that if they managed to get this interloper to the village in one piece it was going to cause quite a stir.

CHAPTER 29

By four o'clock that afternoon the temporary corral at Waterby was thronging with horseflesh. The drift was the one and only time of the year that so many Dartmoor hill and the purebred Dartmoor ponies were seen in one place – usually they were dotted across the moor in their own small herds. Leaning against the rails of the corral were the farmers, also brought together from far flung corners for the annual ritual.

Henry Blossom was taking photographs of the bustling scene while Sniffer Smith chatted to a couple of the older farmers, whose eyes were roving over the ponies looking for their owners' individual marks.

"Remind me, how do you tell who owns which ponies?" Sniffer asked the two farmers, pen poised over his notebook.

"There's some who favour ear cuts and others cut their ponies' tail hair in different patterns, but mine all have ear tags," answered one gruffly.

"'Course, the foals are all born between May and August so they have no mark, but they stick so close to their dams we know which are ours," added the other, eyeing Sniffer with interest as the journalist turned his words into shorthand squiggles on the page of his notebook.

"And what happens now?" Sniffer queried.

"Once we've sorted the ponies they'll go back to their own farms where they'll be checked over and wormed. We'll wean the foals and decide which ponies to send back onto the moor and which to send to market," explained the second farmer.

His companion added, "Aye, it's usually the colts and the older ponies that go to market. The hardiest go back on the moor to breed."

As they talked a whisper went up among the people leaning against the rails. Sniffer - who was hard-wired to detect a good story a mile off - pricked his ears and looked around, trying to identify the reason for all the excited murmuring.

"What's everyone talking about?" he asked the old farmers, who were chuckling quietly to themselves.

"Well, lad, it's not your Beast of Dartmoor, but it's almost as infamous around here," said the first, giving Sniffer a toothy grin before pointing to the latest ponies being driven into the corral by two men on quad bikes. Sniffer stared at the newcomers but all he could see were more of the same. He looked at the two men quizzically.

The second farmer took pity on him. "Look at that grey pony, right at the back of the corral. That's the pony that escaped from George Blackstone's yard all them years ago, that is. Caught at last, the same year Tory Wickens moved out of Riverdale. Funny that," he smirked.

"I don't really see the relevance," said Sniffer. "Perhaps you could enlighten me?" But before the farmer could explain Henry Blossom walked up, told Sniffer it was time they headed back to the office and steered him firmly in the direction of their car, which was parked on a verge nearby. Once the journalist and photographer had driven off down the lane towards Tavistock the two old farmers resumed their ponderings.

"I wonder what old George'll make of it all. He always thought there was cash to be had with that pony and you know how he likes his money-making schemes."

His companion hooted with laughter. "Blackstone's so tight moths fly out of his wallet every time he opens it. But I wouldn't have thought he'll be making much from that one. It'd be kinder to put the poor thing out of its misery, if you asked me."

They both looked at the grey pony standing at the back of the corral. His head low, his ears flat, he exuded exhaustion from every pore. At the other end of the corral farmers had begun sorting their ponies.

As soon as their marks were identified they were sent into smaller pens with a hefty slap on the rump. From the smaller pens they were herded up the ramps of waiting livestock trailers before being transported back to their farms.

"Where is George, anyway?" asked the first farmer, scanning the faces lining the corral for their neighbour.

"Looks like he's sent Jimmy instead," said his companion, pointing to an unassuming-looking lad a few feet away. "Blackstone's probably back at home counting his money and dreaming up his next get rich quick scheme."

"Do you remember that time he tried selling bottled Dartmoor springwater to the tourists?" said the first farmer, taking a pipe out of his pocket and planting it in the corner of his mouth.

"Aye. You mean the water he was getting straight from his kitchen tap? He'd sell the coat from his own mother's back if she was still alive, God love her."

"I hope he does right by that poor pony. You know me, I'm not usually sentimental, but look at it. It hasn't had much of a life, that's for sure."

They both watched as Jimmy, George Blackstone's faithful farm-hand, started driving his employer's ponies into one of the smaller pens. The old bay stallion bore the Blackstone mark, a small nick to the left ear, as did his mares. Jimmy walked behind them, a walking stick in each hand to propel them into the pen. Only once they were all in did Jimmy notice

Cloud for the first time. He'd still been at school when Blackstone had bought the Wickens' pony but remembered the accident. The girl who died had been a pupil at his school, although a few years younger than him. He'd heard how Blackstone had been incandescent with rage when his new purchase had escaped and how, to the farmer's intense annoyance, the pony had somehow managed to evade capture in the drift year after year.

I wonder, he thought to himself. What if this is the famous Cloud Nine? The pony was eyeing him warily. Jimmy had the uncomfortable feeling it was reading his mind. He couldn't see Blackstone's mark so, lunging forward, he tried to grab the pony's left ear. But Cloud was too quick and, with teeth bared, he snaked his head away and squealed in anger. Smarting with humiliation and feeling the eyes of a dozen dour hill farmers on his back Jimmy retreated to the side of the corral to consider his options. He felt stuck between a rock and a hard place. This pony, almost certainly Blackstone's, had plainly gone feral and was going to be a nightmare to get back to the farm. But Jimmy had been on the receiving end of George Blackstone's vicious temper more times than he cared to remember and he had no intention of incurring the farmer's wrath by failing to bring the pony back with the rest of his herd.

Squaring his bony shoulders Jimmy set off once again. Before the pony could react Jimmy raised his walking sticks in the air and roared, "Gerrup you old donkey!"

The two old farmers watching the scene unfold saw a spark of fight flare briefly in the pony's eyes. But as one of Jimmy's sticks connected heavily with the pony's rump the spark died. Acquiescent, Cloud limped into the pen and Jimmy punched the air and whooped in victory. The pony watched defeated as the jubilant farmhand tied the gate tightly shut with a length of orange baler twine.

CHAPTER 30

Dusk was falling as Jimmy drove back to George Blackstone's farm. Cloud and the rest of the ponies stamped restlessly in the back of the lorry as he negotiated the potholed track to the farmyard. The yard was empty. Jimmy swung through the gateposts and parked by the side of an open barn. He jumped out of the cab and strode over to the back door of the farmhouse. His arrival set Blackstone's two border collies off in a frenzy of barking. Tied to a post inside the barn, the dogs strained against their ropes in their eagerness to reach Jimmy, who usually had a treat and a kind word for them.

The Blackstone farm was a gloomy place. It had been a thriving business when George's parents were alive and the yard and farmhouse had been as neat as a pin. But over three decades it had slowly fallen to rack and ruin. George Blackstone was as mean as he was idle, and hadn't spent a penny on the place in years. Buildings were patched together with old timber and hope and the field next to the barn resembled a tractor graveyard, a place where the farm's once fine fleet of vehicles had given up and died.

Jimmy paused for a second by the back door. He hoped Blackstone would be pleased that he'd returned Cloud but you never knew. It had been a long day and the last thing he needed was a tongue-lashing. He rapped on the door and let himself in.

"Jimmy, is that you?" barked a querulous voice from the depths of the old farmhouse. Jimmy's heart sank to the bottom of his mud splattered boots.

"Just coming, Mr Blackstone. And I've a surprise for you!" he replied, shaking off his wellies in the filthy hallway. George Blackstone was sitting by a smoky fire in what had once been his mother's best parlour. But her beloved knick-knacks had long been sold off and the once cream walls were now yellowed with nicotine. A half-drunk bottle of whisky and a dirty glass sat on a small table next to Blackstone's armchair. Jimmy quailed. His boss was a vindictive drunk.

"Did you bring back my ponies?" Blackstone demanded, his sour breath causing Jimmy to gag.

"Yes, Mr Blackstone. And not just the Dartmoor ponies. You'll never guess what else I've got in the back of the lorry!"

"Go on – surprise me," the old man replied.

"You remember that pony you bought off Tory Wickens all them years ago?" Blackstone nodded. It still sent his blood pressure rocketing whenever he thought about the money he'd wasted on that no-good Connemara.

"Well, it was caught in the drift and I've brought it back for you."

It took a moment for the penny to drop but when it did an unpleasant leer spread across his face. Jimmy could almost see the pound signs light up in his rheumy eyes.

"Well, well, that's a turn up for the books," he said, picking up his walking stick and pushing Jimmy roughly out of the way in his haste to see Cloud.

Together they went out into the yard. While Jimmy shut the gate Blackstone let the lorry's ramp down with a clatter. He peered into the dark interior of the lorry but all he could see were half a dozen terrified Dartmoor ponies staring back at him.

"Where is it then?" Blackstone howled. Jimmy rushed over to the lorry, tripping up the ramp in his hurry to herd the ponies out into the yard. Standing at the back of the lorry was Cloud, the whites of his eyes piercing the gloom. Blackstone laughed nastily and followed Jimmy up the ramp.

"Go and see to the others, boy. You can shut the ramp behind me. I need to teach this one a lesson. No-one gets the better of George Blackstone," he said softly.

Jimmy suddenly felt sorry for the dappled grey pony. But his fear of Blackstone was far greater and he turned away from the lorry and did as he was told, flinching as he heard the desperate crack of wood meeting horseflesh.

An hour later George Blackstone's Dartmoor ponies had been fed and watered and were huddled together in the far corner of a small paddock at the rear of the farmhouse. Jimmy had checked them over, paying special attention to the three yearlings he would be driving to the horse sale in Tavistock the next day. He fed the border collies and gave the yard a half-hearted sweep, but his gaze kept returning to the lorry, which stood in the glow cast by the security light above Blackstone's back door.

After the first sickening crunch of wood on horse everything had been silent. Jimmy had gone about his jobs methodically, trying to blot out images of splintered bones and dark weals on once white flanks. But he couldn't put it off any longer. Leaning the broom against the back wall of the farmhouse he walked over to the lorry, clearing his throat nervously as he went.

"Mr Blackstone?" His voice came out croakily and he tried again, louder this time. "Mr Blackstone! Is everything alright in there?"

There was no reply. Jimmy released the ramp and crept up. He stood for a moment trying to see, but the back of the lorry was in complete darkness. He became aware of laboured breathing. "Mr Blackstone, are you OK?"

He remembered the small pen torch on his key ring and grappled around in his trouser pocket until his fingers closed around it. The tiny beam of light was next to useless but Jimmy shone it into the depths of the lorry anyway, praying it would reveal nothing but a lame, bedraggled grey pony and that his boss had gone back into the farmhouse while he was out in the paddock tending to the ponies. His hand was shaking, causing the pinprick of light to dance like a firefly inside the lorry. Jimmy took a deep breath and tried to steady both his hand and his nerves.

But when the light came to rest on a prone body lying on the straw all coherent thoughts vanished. Jimmy opened his lungs and screamed.

CHAPTER 31

Mike McKeever's plane touched down at Heathrow the next day after an uneventful six and a half hour flight. As he and his fellow passengers on board the airbus sat waiting for the seatbelt lights to go off he thought about the last few weeks. It had been a good trip and the programme editor had been pleased with Mike's reports from the front line. He had a natural empathy with both the British soldiers and the local people, which always came across in his pieces. He loved being in the thick of the action and told friends he had the best job in the world. Yet recently he found he was missing Caroline and the children more and more and was beginning to wonder if a desk job back in London might be better for the whole family.

Leaving them for this trip, so soon after the move

to Riverdale, had been a real wrench. Charlie was his father's son and took his dad's work trips in his stride but Caroline, normally so cheerful, had seemed unhappy when he'd left. And there was Poppy. With her pale, heart-shaped face and green eyes she looked so much like Isobel that sometimes it took Mike's breath away. She was skinny, shy and awkward but Mike knew that one day she would be as beautiful as her mother.

From the moment Mike and Isobel had met during a lecture in their first year at university they'd been inseparable and were married within three years of graduating.

They'd had their lives mapped out. They'd both wanted careers – Mike at the BBC and Isobel as a primary school teacher - a family home, four children and a golden retriever. Within a few years they'd had the jobs, the Victorian terrace in Twickenham and, most importantly, Poppy. Mike felt the luckiest man alive. Then life dealt him its worst possible hand.

His grief after Isobel's death had threatened to consume him, but somehow he'd managed to hold everything together for Poppy's sake. Overnight she'd morphed from a confident and carefree four-year-old to a withdrawn, clingy and painfully shy shadow of her former self. Father and daughter had clung to each other like the battered and bruised survivors of a shipwreck.

Slowly the pain had lessened. Mike still missed Isobel acutely but he began to enjoy work again, and sometimes hours went by when she didn't fill his thoughts. Then Caroline had started working in Mike's department and the two had become friends. They were both gregarious and shared the same quirky sense of humour. To the delight of their friends and families they'd fallen in love. The arrival of Charlie was the icing on the cake.

Mike felt so grateful he'd been given a second chance. He wished Poppy felt the same. But no matter how hard Caroline tried Poppy refused to let down her defences. Caroline never complained about Poppy's remoteness and Mike was away so often it was easy to pretend everything was OK. Deep down he knew it was anything but.

The seatbelt light finally went out. Mike stood up, stretched his legs and reached for his hand luggage in the overhead locker. He knew that once he was home he would have to sit down and talk to Poppy about Caroline. Mike had once found an old shoebox filled with photographs of a pony, schedules from long-forgotten gymkhanas and dog-eared rosettes at the bottom of Caroline's wardrobe. His wife had been as pony mad as Poppy was at her age. They had so much in common, if only Poppy was prepared to look.

His taxi driver was a taciturn type so Mike was spared the effort of making small talk on the long drive back to Riverdale. Instead he spent the journey deep in thought, wondering how he could bridge the gap between his wife and daughter.

As they neared Tavistock the traffic slowed to a

crawl and Mike realised they were stuck behind several livestock lorries all heading in the same direction. The taxi driver drummed the steering wheel with his fingers and let out the occasional deep sigh.

"It's like Piccadilly bleedin' Circus around here today," muttered the driver, throwing Mike an accusatory look through the rear view mirror, as if he was personally responsible for the traffic jam. Mike smiled inwardly while trying to look sympathetic. They trundled on for another couple of miles. When they reached the outskirts of the town he saw a sign with the words 'Horse Sale, first left' on the side of the road.

It must be the auction where the Dartmoor ponies were sold, Mike thought. Caroline had mentioned the annual event in an email. Apparently it was quite a spectacle. His mind was racing. He remembered Poppy, white with disappointment when she'd realised there was no pony waiting for her at their new home the day they'd moved to Riverdale. He thought about the emails she'd sent him since, brimming with news about Chester, her new friend Scarlett's two ponies and little else. He pictured Caroline's scruffy shoebox, buried at the bottom of her wardrobe, filled with memories of her own pony-filled childhood.

Mike made a split decision. He tapped the driver on the shoulder, dazzled him with his practised television news smile and, with just the right mix of persuasion and authority, said, "Actually, could you just take a left here? There's somewhere I need to go."

CHAPTER 32

The Tavistock Pony Sale in the town's livestock
centre was the first of the annual drift sales and drew
people from far and wide. Everyone, from the
farmers to the workers running the sale, seemed to
know exactly what they were doing. Mike, still in the
crumpled suit he was wearing when he left the Middle
East, felt distinctly out of place. He picked up a sale
catalogue and studied it carefully, trying to glean as
much information as he could. The sale had started at
ten o'clock and was due to finish at four. He looked
at his watch. Three thirty. He was worried he'd left it
too late. But ponies were still being sent into the ring
one by one. Mike watched as the onlookers cast
critical eyes over the fillies and colts, searching for
good conformation and the potential to make a

decent riding pony. Standing over them all, in a wooden construction that resembled a prison watchtower, was the auctioneer, whose sharp eyes roved keenly over the crowds, so as not to miss a single bid.

The ponies were being sold in guineas. Mike caught the eye of the woman standing to his right. She was wearing a quilted jacket and a headscarf and looked like she might know a thing or two about horses. "Excuse me, I'm new to all this. How much is a guinea?"

"Well, in old money it would have been one pound and one shilling, but these days it's £1.05," she answered, happy to share her knowledge. "Until recently ponies were selling for as little as a couple of guineas. They were worth more dead than alive. So sad. Now there's a minimum price of 10 guineas on every pony."

Mike smiled his thanks and turned back to the ring where a diminutive chestnut foal was trotting obligingly around the ring, its ears pricked and its head held high. The bidding had reached 42 guineas.

"Are you buying or selling?" the woman asked. Her greying brown hair, long face and large front teeth reminded Mike uncannily of Chester.

He shook the thought away and replied, "To be honest, it was a spur of the moment thing. I happened to be passing, saw the sign and thought I'd pop in and have a look."

"I've bought a bay colt for my grandson," she

informed him. "Silly really – Matthew's still in nappies. But by the time he's ready to ride the pony will be rising five. He's a fine looking fellow and should make a terrific riding pony."

"My daughter Poppy's horse mad," said Mike conversationally. "She'd love a pony more than anything else in the world, but I know as much about horses as I do about quantum physics."

"Well, it would be a mistake to buy a foal. Putting two novices together is a recipe for disaster. Much better to buy her a ready-made riding pony, if that's what you were thinking," said the woman.

"I don't really know what I was thinking, if I'm honest," admitted Mike. "But she's been through a tough time and I think it would be good for her."

"I agree. I think pony mad girls deserve their own ponies. But then horses are my thing," said the woman. "I'm Bella, by the way. Bella Thompson."

"Mike McKeever. Nice to meet you," said Mike, extending his hand. "We've not long moved to Devon. We live near Waterby."

"I know the village well. My old friend Tory Wickens used to live there, though I hear she's moved to Tavistock now. Haven't seen her in yonks."

Mike laughed. "It's a small world – we bought Riverdale from Tory at the beginning of the summer. Poppy inherited Tory's old donkey Chester, although it's a pony she'd really like."

"Well I never," replied Bella, pumping Mike's hand vigorously. She had an extraordinarily firm handshake for a woman in her sixties.

They turned to watch another couple of foals take their turn in the ring. The crowd had started to thin out and bidding had slowed right down. Mike checked his watch again. Nearly ten to four and the sale was almost over. He remembered the grumpy taxi driver still sitting outside.

"It was lovely to meet you, Bella, but I'd better be off. You're right – it was a crazy idea to even think about buying a foal for Poppy – she's only eleven. If we're going to get her a pony we should do it properly. Get some proper advice, find something safe for her to ride."

As he spoke the gate into the ring opened to reveal a much bigger pony, twice the size of the foals but with none of their bounce. Receiving a forcible shove from the man at the gate it limped painfully in. Bella, who had been about to give Mike's hand another hearty shake, turned back to the ring, her attention fixed on the pony now hobbling around the inside of the rails. It was what Mike would have called white and Poppy would have said was grey, though it was hard to tell – its hair was matted and streaked with what looked suspiciously like blood.

"Now that, if I'm not much mistaken, was once a top class riding pony, though it's hard to believe it looking at him now," said Bella. "In fact, if I'm right, and I'm pretty sure I am, you might be interested to know that that poor pony once belonged to Riverdale," she continued, turning to Mike with a glint in her eye.

Mike had been about to leave but his interest was piqued. "Belonged to Riverdale? What do you mean?"

"I'm pretty sure that's Cloud Nine, a Connemara pony Tory Wickens bought for her granddaughter Caitlin years ago. He was a beautiful pony and he and Caitlin made an unbeatable team, that is until the accident -"

Bella was interrupted by the auctioneer, whose ringing voice was met with jeers from the handful of people still lining the ring as he attempted to get the bidding started.

"I know we've only just met and you probably think I'm a mad old woman for saying so, but you should bid for that pony. Buy him for your daughter," said Bella.

Mike looked at her, his eyebrows raised. The pony looked half dead as it plodded unevenly around the ring. He shrugged his shoulders. He was beginning to wonder if it was all too much hassle, and turned to go.

"Trust me. Just start bidding!" said Bella urgently, tugging his sleeve.

Mike looked at the pony again. Head nodding with every painful step as he limped around the sale ring, he looked as though he'd lost the will to live. Could this sorry excuse for a pony really be the answer he'd been looking for, a shared interest to bring Caroline and Poppy together? Deciding he had nothing to lose, Mike reluctantly raised his hand and tried to catch the auctioneer's eye. He remembered what Bella had told him about the minimum sale price and said in a loud voice, which sounded more confident than he felt, "Ten guineas."

A man wearing dirty blue overalls standing opposite them immediately bid eleven, and when Mike raised his hand again there was a ripple of laughter.

"You're bidding against the knackerman!" hissed Bella. "Keep going!"

The next couple of minutes passed in a blur of bid and counter bid. Mike felt confident that he could outbid the man from the slaughterhouse, and he was starting to picture Poppy's delight when he brought the pony home to Riverdale. But just as he was about to raise his hand for what he was certain would be the winning bid a man with a weasel-like face standing to his left dropped a bombshell.

"I'd save your money if I were you, mate. Did you know that animal killed a girl?"

"*What?*" demanded Mike. He stopped bidding and turned his full attention to the man.

"It's a bad 'un, you mark my words. The knacker's yard is the best place for it, if you ask me."

"I didn't ask you," Mike replied icily and turned back to the ring.

But it was too late. The sale had been made. The grey pony had disappeared and the auctioneer had already moved on to the next lot.

CHAPTER 33

Poppy was lying on her bed, her chin cupped in her hands and a riding magazine open on the duvet in front of her, trying to pass the time until her dad arrived home. She'd barely glanced at the magazine. When she wasn't staring morosely out of the window at the darkening sky, she was watching the minute hand of the old Mickey Mouse alarm clock on her bedside table. The harder she looked at the dial, the slower the hand seemed to move. Her dad had been due home at four o'clock. It was now half past, and there was still no sign of him.

Poppy looked down at the magazine. It was open on a feature about first aid for ponies. 'How to save your pony's life!' ran the headline. She scanned the top ten things to include in a first aid kit and she skim-read the tips on treating wounds and common causes of lameness. Everything she saw, read or heard

made her think of Cloud. She knew in her heart that
he would never have been able to outrun the drift and
by now was almost certainly back at George
Blackstone's farm. The thought chilled her to the
core.

Twenty five to five and her dad was still a no-show.
Poppy could make out the sound of Caroline singing
along to a song on the radio in the kitchen. Knowing
Caroline, she was probably dancing around the
kitchen table, too, and the thought made Poppy smile.
She and Caroline had had a heart to heart earlier, just
the two of them. Poppy had been mucking out
Chester and Caroline had come to see if she needed
any help. They chatted easily now and Poppy no
longer felt awkward around her stepmother. For the
first time she could remember they'd talked about
Isobel, and it had been OK. Better than OK, in fact –
it had been good. As she looked over to the clock
again her eyes fell on the photo of her mum. Poppy
still missed her deeply, but she no longer felt so alone.

The distant rumble of a lorry interrupted her
thoughts. It was a welcome distraction and she flung
the magazine on the floor. The rumble grew louder
and was followed by the crunch of tyres on gravel.

"Dad's home!" yelled Charlie at the top of his
voice, and Poppy could feel the walls of the old house
tremble as he galloped along the landing and down
the stairs. By the time she reached the hallway Charlie
had already flung open the front door. She had been
expecting a taxi but was flummoxed to see a sleek

horsebox parked outside.

"That's weird," she said, half to herself. The horsebox was steel grey with a berry red logo. Poppy could just make out the words Redhall Manor Equestrian Centre. It was probably trying to reach the farm but had taken the wrong track, she thought. Then the passenger door opened and her dad jumped out. Charlie whooped and ran into his outstretched arms. Poppy waited a heartbeat and followed. Her dad's suit was crumpled and there were shadows under his eyes but his face was tanned and he was grinning from ear to ear.

"Come here and give your tired old dad a hug, kids," he commanded.

"Mike!" called Caroline from the front door. She stopped in her tracks when she saw the horsebox. "What on earth -?"

"I cadged a lift with Ted in Tavistock," Mike said, gesturing at the driver, who was also jumping down from the cab. "We got delayed for one reason or another and my taxi driver had another airport run to do. I bumped into Ted and he said he was coming this way and would give me a lift in return for a cup of tea."

They all filed into the house, congregating in the kitchen where Caroline made tea. Mike looked at his daughter, who was offering everyone a slice of coffee cake. She was growing up so fast. "Be an angel and go and get my hand luggage out of the horsebox, Poppy. It's in the groom's compartment, through the door on the side. There's a light switch on the left, I think. There might be something for you both in there," he added, winking at Charlie, who whooped again. As she crossed the gravel to the lorry she heard him yell after her. "Poppy! I nearly forgot. Your present might be harder to spot. Just keep looking and I'm sure you'll find it."

She walked around to the far side of the lorry and let herself in, feeling in the darkness for the light switch. After a couple of sweeps of the wall she found the switch, flicked it on and looked around curiously. She'd seen plenty of horseboxes in her pony magazines but had never been inside one. Scarlett just had a trailer on the farm, which her dad towed behind his old Land Rover. The groom's accommodation reminded her of the inside of a caravan. There was a small sink and draining board with cupboards and a tiny fridge underneath, a sleeping area over the cab and a long seat the length of the wall opposite the door.

On the seat was the battered, black suitcase her dad used as hand luggage. Next to it was a carrier bag with the barrel of the biggest Nerf gun Poppy had ever seen poking out of the top. Charlie would be beyond excited. She walked over, picked both bags up and put them by the door. Poppy looked around her again. Her dad's big suitcase was by the sink. She tried lifting it but it was so heavy she could barely haul it an inch off the ground. He'd have to come and get it later. There was no sign of any other bags but as

Poppy turned to go she noticed the interior door that led to the horse area. She paused. Ted hadn't said if he had any horses in the back but it wouldn't do any harm to poke her nose through the door and have a look, would it?

"Of course it wouldn't!" she exclaimed, her voice sounding unnaturally loud in the empty space. There was a thump from the horse area and a low noise that sounded very much like a whicker. Poppy reached for the door handle.

The light from the groom's area revealed the first of three padded partitions which stood at an angle to the sides of the lorry. Peering around the partition she saw a Dartmoor foal, blinking nervously behind a hay net that was almost as big as he was. Poppy smiled and went to stroke his nose, but he shrank from her touch. "Don't worry, little fellow. I'm not going to hurt you. I just wanted to say hello. Are you all on your own?"

At the sound of her voice there was another whicker from the stall next to the foal. Poppy felt the hairs on her neck stand up. She hardly dared to look at the foal's companion but when she did she gasped. Standing with his legs slightly splayed was a skeletal grey pony. He looked as insubstantial as a wraith, but when he turned his brown eyes to Poppy they burned with life. "Cloud!" Poppy breathed. She flung her arms around his bony neck and he stood patiently while she sobbed noisily, snot mingling with the sweat and dried blood in his tangled mane.

Minutes passed as they stood locked together. Poppy's mind was reeling. Could Cloud be for her? But how had her dad known about him – she'd never mentioned him in any of her emails. And anyway, things like that only happened in stories, not to girls like her.

More likely Cloud was destined for the flash-sounding Redhall Manor Equestrian Centre where he would be used as a riding pony for spoilt rich kids. But at least he was safe from the brutal hands of George Blackstone. Poppy realised that was all that mattered.

She hugged him fiercely. "I'll find out where you're going and I will always look out for you, Cloud," she muttered into his mane.

"No need for that. He's staying right here," said a cheerful voice. She looked up and saw Ted opening the ramp of the horsebox.

"But I don't understand –", she gulped, wiping her nose on the sleeve of her jumper.

"Your dad bought him at the pony sale in Tavistock this afternoon. My boss offered the lorry to bring him back to Riverdale. He's as thin as a stick and very nervy but you two seem to have made friends already!"

Mike and Caroline were standing at the bottom of the ramp, arms around each other, broad smiles on their faces.

"It's Cloud!" Poppy told her stepmother, the disbelief on her face giving way to joy.

Caroline's blue eyes were sparkling. "I thought it might be from the way your dad described him."

"But Daddy, how did you *know*?"

"I'd like to take the credit but I'm afraid it was all down to Ted's boss, Bella. We bumped into each other at the pony sale this afternoon. She's a force to be reckoned with, I tell you." Ted chuckled at the accurate description of his boss as he undid the first two partitions of the horsebox.

"I was looking for a foal for you but Bella said no, two novices together would be a mistake. Then this one walked into the ring and Bella reckoned he would be perfect for you, Poppy. He looked like a mess to me but she sounded so sure I found myself bidding. It was me against the knackerman," said Mike succinctly. Poppy shuddered.

"Then a man standing next to us told me the pony had killed a girl. I didn't know whether to believe him or not. But before I had a chance to ask Bella if it was true the bidding was over. Someone had bought him."

Poppy held her breath as her dad continued. "It was Bella. She told me he belonged to Riverdale and that I could pay her back later. And suddenly I was the owner of a dappled grey bag of bones with a notorious reputation and not much else. I had no idea you two had already met," Mike finished, looking at his tear-streaked daughter. She was leaning heavily against Cloud, while he rested his head on her slight shoulder. It gave the illusion that they were propping each other up.

"I don't understand how he ended up at the pony sale. I thought George Blackstone would have wanted to keep him," said Poppy.

"I can answer that," answered Ted. "Apparently he came off the moor yesterday afternoon in the drift near Waterby."

Poppy and Caroline nodded. They'd guessed that much.

"He was taken back to Blackstone's farm. Blackstone's a miserable old sod who lives on the other side of the village," Ted explained to Mike. "According to gossip, Blackstone went into the back of his lorry with the pony. Who knows what he intended to do but knowing Blackstone it wasn't to give the pony a titbit. His farmhand Jimmy found Blackstone a while later. He'd fallen and knocked himself out. He was out cold for quite a while, apparently. Jimmy had to slap his cheeks a few times before he came round. Other than a blinding headache he was as right as rain. Unfortunately." Ted added with feeling.

Poppy looked at the streaks of dried blood that were caked to Cloud's flanks and wondered what had gone on in the back of that lorry. She laid her cheek gently against Cloud's as Ted continued. "Blackstone decided last night to send the pony to the sales. He wasn't prepared to throw good money after bad, Jimmy said. Cloud here was one of the last lots of the afternoon. Bella recognised him as soon as he came into the ring. And the rest you know. Right, shall we unload him now?"

Poppy pulled the quick release knot and led Cloud slowly down the ramp and around the back of the house to the stables. As she passed the kitchen window she saw Charlie watching her, a huge grin on his face. Her heart was threatening to burst as she undid the bolts of Chester's stable. The donkey looked up and hee-hawed loudly when he saw his old friend. Cloud limped straight over and they nuzzled each other affectionately.

"It's a bit of a squeeze. Do you think they'll be OK in there together?" asked Caroline, who was watching over the stable door.

Poppy looked at them and smiled. "I think so. He looks pretty settled already, I'd say."

"We'll get the vet out to have a look at his leg. You do realise it's going to be a long journey, getting him back to full strength, Poppy? His leg might be so badly damaged you'll never be able to ride him. And if it does heal it's been years since Cloud has had anyone on his back. We'll be starting from scratch," said Caroline.

Poppy was glad her stepmother was planning to help. It felt right.

"I know, Mum. All I care about is that he's safe and he's here. Anything else will be a bonus."

Caroline smiled. Cloud Nine lay down, exhausted, in the thick straw, with Chester standing over him as if keeping guard.

They knew they had a long road ahead of them, but they would travel it together. All that really mattered was that Cloud had finally come home.

ABOUT THE AUTHOR

Amanda Wills was born in Singapore and grew up in the Kent countryside surrounded by a menagerie of animals including four horses, three cats, a dog and numerous sheep, rabbits and chickens.

She worked as a journalist for more than 20 years and is now a police press officer.

Three years ago Amanda combined her love of writing with her passion for horses and began writing pony fiction. Her first novel, The Lost Pony of Riverdale, was published in 2013. The sequel, Against all Hope, followed in the summer of 2014 and the third in the series, Into the Storm, was published in January 2015.

The Riverdale Stories are currently being translated into Norwegian, Swedish and Finnish.

Find out more at www.amandawills.co.uk or like The Riverdale Stories on Facebook.

Printed in Great Britain
by Amazon